Romance Unbound Publishing
Presents

Sold into Slavery

Claire Thompson

Edited by
Jae Ashley
Donna Fisk

Cover Design by Kelly Shorten

Print ISBN 9781475267662
Copyright 2012 Claire Thompson
All rights reserved

Chapter 1

"Don't I know you from somewhere?"

Devin Lyons stood over the lovely blond, aware the line sounded hackneyed, even though it was true. Something about the girl *was* familiar, though he couldn't say precisely what. She was lying on her stomach, her head buried in a book, her bikini top untied. Her tan skin was oiled, and the scent of cocoa butter mingled with the salty sea air.

From his position on a towel a few feet away, he'd been surreptitiously admiring the sweet rise of her small, round ass, barely covered by a tiny red bikini, and the curve of her bare breast pressed against the beach towel.

The young woman squinted up at him. Tilting her head, she regarded him a moment with dark blue eyes. "I don't think so," she said.

"Forgive me. When I travel abroad, I tend to run into all sorts of people. You look like someone I once knew. I apologize for the intrusion." He knew he should leave it at that and quit bothering the young woman, but he couldn't quite bring himself to walk away. She was *so* lovely.

Shading her eyes with her hand, she continued to stare up at him, a small smile now playing over her face. "You're British, aren't you? I love the accent."

This was almost invariably what American women said to Devin upon first meeting him, and he was aware it gave him an instant advantage over the American blokes, an advantage he wasn't above seizing. He smiled, nodding. "From London. And you're American."

"Guilty as charged." The girl reached behind herself, tying the string of her bikini top into a little bow. Lifting herself into a sitting position, she patted the towel beside her. "Want to sit? The sun is behind you—it makes it hard to see your face."

Devin sat down beside her on the large towel, thinking with some amazement he was in the process of picking someone up, something he rarely, if ever did. He couldn't seem to tear his eyes away from hers, and she, instead of looking away, stared back.

"Oh," she said softly, her lips forming a small, pink O, as if she was surprised. A faint blush moved over her cheeks, her hand moving to cover the pendant of her necklace.

"Forgive me," Devin finally managed. "I don't mean to stare." Yet his eyes remained fastened on her face, drinking her in as if she were water, and he a man dying of thirst.

Suddenly the girl gave a small laugh and shook back her hair, as if released from a spell. She let go of the pendant and, as Devin's eye was drawn down to necklace, a jolt of excited recognition moved through him. The interlocking links of the chain were thick, and from it hung a small padlock.

Deeply intrigued, Devin murmured, "That necklace—it's quite unusual."

"Thank you," the girl replied, though he hadn't necessarily meant his remark as a compliment.

Devin continued to stare at the padlock dangling from its chain. Could that be a slave collar around her neck, a talisman of erotic ownership by another? Was that what had so attracted him to her from the instant he'd laid eyes on her? Was there some kind of silent, pheromone-type signal between a Dom and a sub that whispered just below the surface of conscious thought, drawing him to her like a bee to honey?

Finally he dared, "Is that something more than just a necklace?" He realized as he asked that he was of two minds. If she said yes, that could mean she was in a committed BDSM relationship, and if she stared uncomprehendingly at him, it could be she was clueless about BDSM or, worse, one of those straitlaced, uptight Americans who would be horrified by the thought of anything beyond the pale of traditional sex.

She regarded him with a bemused expression, finally saying, "I don't even know your name, Mr. Brit. Mine is Leah. Leah Jacobs." She held out her hand. Her fingers were long and slender, her wrists delicate. But as he took the offered hand, her grip was firm.

"Forgive my rudeness," he said at once. "My name is Lyons. Devin Lyons. I work for an international estate agency that has business in Thailand. It's a pleasure to meet you, Leah Jacobs." He realized he was holding her hand a bit too long, and reluctantly let her go.

"What brings you to Pattaya?" he asked, to prevent himself from pulling her close and crushing her lips with his. When had he last been so utterly and completely captivated?

"I'm traveling with a charter tour group," Leah replied. "Pattaya is one of the stops on our whirlwind tour of Thailand and Vietnam. I didn't realize they have such nice beaches here."

Devin nodded his agreement. This particular stretch of beach was owned by the hotel at which he was staying, the Pattaya Gold, and was reserved for its patrons, most of whom were European and American. When he glanced sidelong at her, Leah was staring out at the sparkling ocean, again fingering the small padlock at her throat.

"That necklace," he began again. "I hope you won't think me too forward if I ask the significance of the lock and chain."

She turned toward him, and he felt the challenge in those impossibly blue eyes. "It was once a slave collar," she said, lifting her chin as she clutched the small lock. Abruptly she dropped it, frowning. "It no longer has meaning to me, at least not specific meaning. The man who gave it to me is out of the picture. I just wear it because…" she paused, and Devin saw a flash of pain moving over her features, but in a second it was gone. She gave a small shrug. "I guess because I like it."

Though Devin had had his share of dealings with Americans, it never ceased to amaze him how direct they could be. No dancing around the topic, as he'd been prepared to do. He decided to reply as directly as she had. "I'm certain the loss was entirely his," he offered. "You are a lovely woman."

She shrugged again. "I thought I was in love with him, but then I found out I didn't know him at all." She wrinkled her nose, adding, "Or the wife and kids that went with him."

Devin tried to look sympathetic, though he was delighted to know she was not only submissive, but available. He noted then the sparkle in her eyes, and after a moment, her lips curled into a charming smile, and Devin smiled back.

She grabbed her long, shiny hair and twisted it like a coil of golden rope, before dropping it again over her shoulder. Her smile edged into a grin as she added, "He did me a favor, the rat bastard. His back was hairy. He smacked his lips when he ate. And he snored." She started to laugh, and Devin found himself laughing with her.

It wasn't that her remarks were especially witty or amusing—it was more the impish spark in her eyes, and the simple, easy happiness Devin felt in her presence. Once the laughter started, neither seemed able to stop. Each time one of them began to sober up, the other would start again. They laughed a long time, the kind of deep belly laughs that leave you with tears streaming down your cheeks.

Finally Leah, wiping her eyes with the back of her hand, said suddenly, "You look like Sean Connery, did you know that? Not the *Indiana Jones'* father Sean Connery, but the young, sexy *James Bond* Sean Connery from the old movies. I thought it immediately when you said, "Lyons. Devin Lyons, just like he used to do."

She sat up straight, saying in a rather excellent impersonation of Sean Connery, "Bond. James Bond." Devin grinned. He wanted to scoop this lovely, fresh girl into his arms and take her immediately to his hotel suite. Recalling himself, he glanced at his watch and cursed softly.

"What is it?" Leah asked.

"Bloody hell," Devin replied. "I have a dinner meeting I have to attend. I need to get back and shower and clean up. I'd so much rather invite you for a drink at the hotel pool, and then…" He let this last bit linger, as he imagined Leah, stripped bare of the red bikini, tied in ropes and ready for him to plunder.

Leah began to pack her bottle of water and suntan lotion. "I have to get back too. I promised to meet some of the women from the group at a little seafood place one of them discovered. Maybe after?"

"Yes, yes," Devin said quickly. "That would be splendid. How about," he looked at his watch again, calculating how long he would have to spend with the businessmen to wrap up the deal, "eight-thirty this evening? We could meet in the bar of the hotel."

Leah nodded, standing. "That should work." She wrapped a yellow sarong over her slender hips while Devin tried not to stare with his tongue hanging out at her gorgeous body. He stood, hoping his rising erection wasn't too obvious in his swim trunks.

"Until this evening."

~*~

"You clean up nice," Leah quipped as she drank in the sight of the tall, sexy Brit. He had looked good enough to eat back on the beach, his smooth, tan chest bare, his shoulders broad, his wavy, light brown hair falling over tawny brown eyes. Now, dressed in a crisp white linen shirt, the sleeves rolled up over his muscular forearms, he was still sexy, but with an added elegance. His black pants fit perfectly, and Leah tried not to stare at his long legs and the sexy bulge at his crotch as he stood.

"Why thank you, ma'am," Devin answered in a terrible approximation of a Texas accent, doffing an imaginary cowboy hat. "You don't look so bad yourself." Leah had spent the last frantic half-hour trying on and taking off every outfit she'd packed for the trip, finally settling on the batik cotton ankle-length skirt she'd gotten in India, along with a dark blue silk tank top.

She smiled and slid onto the barstool beside Devin. After ordering a lime daiquiri, Leah turned to Devin. "So, all your business dealings squared away?"

Devin nodded. "Just about in the bag. A few more loose ends to tie up."

"And then, what? Back to the UK?" She tried to tell herself she didn't care, but she did.

"That's the plan. Though I have a little vacation time coming. I was actually thinking of staying on a while longer here in Pattaya. And yourself?"

The bartender set Leah's drink before her. She cradled the cold glass between her hands, trying not to betray her excitement that he would be around a while. "The group I'm traveling with is scheduled to leave the day after tomorrow. We're going on to Bangkok. But I have flexibility. As long as I don't miss the charter flight home, I can pretty much do what I want."

Devin took a long pull of his beer and Leah admired his strong profile as he drank. He set down the bottle and turned to her. "Excellent. I do hope we get the chance to know one another better." He swiveled on the barstool to face her. His eyes were amber, she decided, dappled with flecks of gold, sparkling in his tan face. Leah felt herself falling into those tawny, golden eyes.

He reached for the padlock on her necklace, gripping it lightly between his finger and thumb. His touch against her throat caused a shudder to run through Leah's frame and she felt her nipples hardening.

When he'd asked about the collar, she'd just blurted out the truth, as surprised as he must have been by her frankness. She'd been devastated when she'd discovered Todd, the man she'd been involved with for nearly a year, and lavished with her submissive trust and devotion, had turned out to be married with two small children.

For some reason, though she refused to see Todd again or listen to his bullshit excuses, she continued to wear the collar, touching it often throughout the day, taking comfort from the cool, heavy metal around her neck. While she no longer loved the man who had given it to her, she loved its symbolism and the promise it had once held for her. She knew she should take it off—it had been six months since Todd's betrayal had come to light—but for some reason she hadn't been ready to give up the last vestige of the relationship. She had loved being owned.

Devin's hand still on the padlock, he leaned close to her, saying softly, "There is something especially lovely about the look of chain against a slender throat. Would you agree?"

As he spoke, he traced the line of the chain, his finger moving sensually along Leah's skin. Again she shuddered involuntarily, feeling heat surge into her cheeks. "I—I," she stuttered, trying to get a hold of herself.

Devin smiled, a lazy, sensual smile that belied the sudden fire in his eyes. Leah could sense the power behind his expression, coiled like a panther ready to spring. His hand still on her throat, Devin leaned closer, his thigh touching hers.

"I know we've only just met, but on some level I feel as if I already know you. As if I've always known you."

Though a part of Leah tried to tell herself this was just an old pickup line, she found herself believing him, as she'd felt the same way from the instant she'd seen him staring down at her on the beach, outlined in gold from the sun.

She went so far as to open her mouth, ready to quip that she'd heard that line before, but when he touched her cheek, drawing two fingers along her skin, the words died in her throat. His fingers moved down past the chain, tracing the line of her collarbone and Leah had to press her lips together to keep from moaning.

Just then two men settled onto the empty barstools on her other side, bumping her shoulder as they loudly called for a drink. Devin dropped his hand, and Leah shook her head, feeling as if she'd just awoken from a dark, sensual dream. She reached for her glass, taking a long drink of the tangy rum and lime.

Devin pushed himself from his stool and stood. Reaching for their drinks, he said, "Let's move to a booth." It wasn't a question, and it didn't occur to Leah to refuse.

She followed him to an empty booth in a dark corner of the large bar. She slid onto a leather-covered padded bench on one side of the booth, expecting Devin to sit across from her, but instead he sat beside her, setting the drinks down in front of them.

They were quiet for a few moments. Leah was keenly aware of Devin's strong, sexy body so close to hers. He smelled good, exuding a clean, masculine scent that made her want to nuzzle her nose against his neck. Not quite daring to do this, instead she lay her head lightly against his shoulder.

"It's not often," Devin said softly, "I meet a woman with whom I feel such an immediate and intense connection. I'd be lying if I didn't admit I want to take you up to my suite right this minute and have my wicked way with you."

Leah said nothing. This sounded pretty good to her too, though a small voice of reason warned her to slow down. Devin continued, "I sense your passion, Leah, and your submissive desire. Just as I'm hardwired to take erotic control, you are hardwired to relinquish it." He paused before adding, "To the right man."

"To the right man," Leah echoed, his words sending a jolt of aching desire directly to her pussy. She was glad of the darkness in the booth, and the fact they were staring straight ahead, rather than at each other.

"You crave the sensual eroticism of rope, and the kiss of a leather whip to heighten the experience," Devin continued in his lovely, rich accent.

"Yes." She nearly whimpered with longing. How was it this man she'd only just met seemed to know her deepest secrets?

"D/s is like a fire, Leah. Fire, not handled properly, can cause damage. There's a thrill there, a flirtation with danger as you take it to the edge. Part of the dance is getting close to that fire without being burned."

"Oh," Leah breathed, the word pulled from deep inside her, her entire body thrumming with anticipation. Devin placed his hand on Leah's thigh. She could feel the warmth of it through the light fabric of her skirt. Lifting her head, Leah started to turn toward him, her lips actually tingling with the need of a kiss, but Devin stopped her.

"Don't move." His voice was gentle but sure, brooking no disobedience. "Keep your eyes straight ahead, hands on the table." It didn't occur to Leah to refuse. He moved his hand slowly down her thigh and calf. She felt him gather the hem of her skirt and then slip his hand beneath it, his fingers now moving slowly up her bare leg.

"I sensed your strength the moment we met," he said. "Submission is not about weakness, but rather about courage, the courage to recognize and embrace what and who you are at the very core of your being." His hand moved up her leg, coming to rest on her bare thigh beneath the table.

Leah blew out a breath, his words electrifying her as much as his touch. She let her legs fall open, unable to exert even the slightest self-control. Her panties were soaking wet, her pussy tingling. Devin's hand inched closer and Leah bit her lip to keep from begging.

She turned her face abruptly to his. "Kiss me," she demanded.

Devin obliged, dipping his head to hers, his lips soft and warm. He slipped his tongue into her mouth and she felt herself melting against him. He took his hand from her thigh and Leah wanted to grab it back. She wanted him to put his hand into her panties. She twisted toward him, aware someone might see, but too turned on to care.

He was the first to pull away from the kiss. Leah opened her eyes, her body leaning into his, her breath coming in rapid pants. Devin slid out of the booth and held out his hand. Leah put her hand in his, allowing him to pull her upright.

He put his arm around her as he led her from the bar. They didn't speak as they waited at the bank of elevators. His arm still around her shoulders, Devin led Leah into an empty car and pushed the button for the top floor of the fourteen-story hotel.

When it glided open, he led her past several doors that lined the narrow hallway. He stopped in front of the last door and slipped his card key into the lock. Pushing open the door, he gestured for Leah to enter in front of him.

Unlike her cramped economy room, with its single bed and a bathroom that barely had room for its toilet and shower stall, Devin had a suite of rooms, including a large, furnished sitting area, a master bedroom and a bathroom with a full-size Jacuzzi.

"Wow," Leah said, lifting her arms and whirling around in a circle. "The penthouse suite, huh?"

Devin smiled. "I've got an expense account. Comes in handy."

It occurred to Leah she'd just allowed herself to be brought up to a strange man's rooms, and not a soul knew where she was. Would she be found the next morning, strangled and stabbed to death, stuffed in the laundry hamper?

She knew even as this thought flitted through her mind that it was nonsense. She'd felt such a strong connection with Devin. And beneath the undeniable sexual attraction, there was a deep, innate sense of trust. She *knew*, on a gut level, that she could trust this man.

He was watching her, a small smile on his face. "It's not often I bring a young woman to my room after only a few hours' acquaintance," he said, as if privy to her thoughts.

"Afraid I'll be too much for you?" she quipped, grinning.

"Quite the contrary," he growled in a low, sexy voice, as he moved suddenly toward her, wrapping her in a strong embrace. Bending her back, he kissed her, all the pent-up passion they'd shared at the bar spilling over into that kiss. He moved her toward the bed as they kissed, finally falling over her and pressing her into the mattress with his body.

If either had thought about taking it slow, their hunger for each other made it impossible. Their hands were moving in a frenzy, tugging, pulling, unbuttoning and unzipping as they lifted hips and shrugged shoulders in their eagerness to feel skin on skin.

When they were both naked, Devin fell on her again, his kiss voracious, his cock hard as steel against her thigh. He lifted his head, lowering it to find her nipple, which he took between his teeth, lightly pulling and then sucking, while Leah moaned her approval. She could feel the wet, swollen throb of her cunt, and ached to feel him inside her.

Lifting himself from her, Devin scooted down, pressing her thighs apart with strong hands. "Ahhh," Leah sighed, the word pulled from her when his tongue made contact with her labia, licking in a teasing circle around her clit. She reached for his head to guide him, and was momentarily startled when she felt the grip of his fingers circling her wrists. As he continued to lick and suckle at her sex, he pressed her wrists firmly to the mattress, making it very clear who was in charge.

Leah felt the sweet heat of submissive surrender settle over her like a silken blanket as Devin held her down. He brought her quickly to a series of orgasms that made her cry out with blinding pleasure.

As she came slowly out of her swoon, she was aware of his mouth still on her—light, sweet kisses on her labia and along her inner thighs. He looked up from between her legs, his hair tousled and falling into those golden brown eyes, a soft smile on his face.

"Beautiful girl," he whispered. "You taste sweet as honey."

She smiled back, feeling as lazy and content as a cat. She watched as Devin stood, and the sight of his huge erection stoked the smoldering embers of her desire. She lifted herself onto her elbows as he moved toward the bureau. She recognized from his movements that he was putting on a condom.

When he turned around, he was holding something. Leah's eyes widened as she took in the black leather bullwhip, dangling like a promise from its braided handle.

"Oh," she gasped, her sexual stupor burning quickly away. It took skill and care to handle one of those properly, and the fact Devin owned one made it pretty clear he was an expert in the delicious, dark art of BDSM.

"You know what this is?" he asked softly as he advanced upon her, his large, thick erection leading the way.

"A bullwhip," she whispered in reply.

"That's right." Devin set it down on the bed beside her. "I want to use it on you, if you prove yourself worthy."

"Oh," she said again, language for the moment abandoning her. She could almost feel the wonderful, fiery sting of its tip, and hear the sonic crack as it made contact with that part of her that longed for erotic pain.

"But first," he whispered, settling himself over her. "I must have you."

He reached for her wrists, guiding them up over her head and pressing them into the mattress as he nudged her still-wet entrance with the head of his sheathed cock. He moved carefully, entering her slowly, his gold-flecked gaze burning into her.

Leah tried to keep her eyes open as he eased inside her. She could feel her muscles contracting around his shaft and she groaned with pleasure as he began to move inside her. She focused on his face for as long as she could, loving the feel of his fingers curled around her wrists and his strong, muscular body over hers as he moved sensually inside her.

Finally she gave up, letting her eyelids flutter shut as she arched up into him, embracing the pleasure radiating from her groin as it flowed over her body. He let her wrists go and threw his head back as he thrust hard inside her. His skin was hot, his neck flushing red as he orgasmed. Leah wrapped her legs around him and held him close in her arms, pulling him deep inside as she lifted her body to meet his.

Afterward they lay still for a long time, his cock still buried in her warmth, their heartbeats tumbling over each other as their breathing slowly eased. Leah drifted in and out of a sexual lethargy, stunned at the intensity of what she'd just experienced.

Eventually Devin rolled from her onto his back. Reaching for her, he pulled her close, guiding her head until she rested it on his chest. As she lay in the comfort and safety of his arms, something surged through Leah, reenergizing her and making her body feel light, as if she could fly. It was, she realized with sudden, startled recognition, joy.

Pure joy.

Her eyes landed on the bullwhip, which lay curled like a sleeping snake on the sheets beside them. She reached for it, stroking the deceptively soft leather. Tilting her head to look into Devin's handsome face, she asked, "So, what's the verdict? Am I worthy?"

His smile told her everything she needed to know.

Chapter 2

Leah wiped the sweat from her forehead with the back of her hand. Though it was only March, the day had dawned hot and wet, the temperature already over ninety degrees. While it had felt pleasant enough when lying on the beach with the sea breeze keeping her cool, here in the heart of the old shopping district with its close, narrow streets and throngs of people was another story.

She touched the V at the hollow of her neck, feeling the lack there, and it made her smile. She was well and truly over Todd Benjamin. He was just a memory, and a fading one, at that.

She'd spent the entire night in Devin's arms. They'd made love again at dawn, this time taking it slower, exploring each other's bodies with passion and tenderness. As Devin held her close, he whispered his promise that soon she would experience the stinging kiss of the whip and the sensual, hot comfort of binding rope.

She'd slept deeply after that, not waking until after nine. When she'd reached for her new lover, she'd been dismayed to find the bed was empty and Devin nowhere in sight. He'd left her a note, written in a strong, masculine hand on the hotel's stationery:

Darling Leah,

I couldn't bring myself to wake you, as you look so beautiful lying there asleep, with that

soft smile on your lips that I like to imagine I put there! I have to spend a dreary day with

stodgy old businessmen, but I should be back in time for dinner. Feel free to order room

service. I can't wait to see you again, lovely girl. If we don't connect sooner,

meet me in the bar at 7:00. I do hope you are free for dinner and then...

With wonderful, wicked thoughts of what I'm going to do to you, Devin

Though she would have rather spent the morning in Devin's arms, Leah contented herself with a breakfast of freshly squeezed orange juice and hot rolls with butter and jam, after which she took a long, steamy soak in Devin's hot tub. While in the tub, she'd removed the slave collar, no longer wanting someone else's chain around her neck, even if it had lost its original meaning. She'd dropped it into the bathroom trashcan, wondering why she'd worn it for so long.

When she finally headed back to her own room it was nearly one o'clock in the afternoon. Surveying her meager wardrobe, she decided she would buy a few new things—something nice for their dinner date, and definitely something sexy for the promised, "*and then…*" in his note.

Now Leah scanned the signs along the storefronts, weaving her way past the crowds as she looked for the jewelry and gem shop the concierge at the hotel had recommended. Again she touched her throat, thinking perhaps she'd find a pretty new necklace for herself, and maybe some gifts for friends and family back home.

At first she'd been a little surprised the concierge had pushed the jewelry store so hard when she'd asked about clothing boutiques. She figured probably a family member owned it, which would explain why the guy had been so eager to show her the glossy color brochure featuring *the finest jewels and gemstones available at the most reasonable prices.* "Tell them Jao sent you, and I can guarantee you will get the best price. They'll know you're not just any tourist, but an experienced traveler, with a good eye for a bargain. Let me know when you're going," he'd said eagerly. "I'll call ahead so they'll be ready with the finest gems, the ones they keep in the back for their best customers."

Armed with Jao's directions and a promise from him that she'd find the jewels of her dreams, she finally spied the storefront with the neatly lettered sign in the window. *Glorious Gemstones and Jewels* was written in English, with Thai lettering beneath it. She pushed opened the door, causing bells to tinkle as she entered the small shop.

It was a long, narrow room, the interior dark and cool compared to the muggy outside air. As her eyes adjusted to the dimness, she saw the place was filled with glass cases displaying all kinds of jewelry, from gaudy gold chains and cheap watches, to wedding band sets and ropes of pearls, to loose gemstones in vibrant reds, greens, blues and amber.

"May I help you?" A small Thai woman in a brightly colored silk dress stood behind one of the counters.

"I'm Leah Jacobs, a friend of Jao's," Leah offered, curious how this would be received.

"Ah, yes, I have been expecting you." The woman smiled, bobbing her head in an eager nod. "I am delighted to make your acquaintance. Jao mentioned you are no mere tourist, but a woman of some culture and experience, a woman who knows the value of fine gemstones."

While this was probably an exaggeration, Leah was pleased Jao had played her up like this. Hopefully it meant she'd get better treatment and be offered higher quality goods than the run-of-the-mill tourist. She smiled, saying casually, "I'm just looking."

"Of course." The woman nodded. "Our best quality items are in the back of the store. The selection out here is for the tourists."

I knew it, Leah thought triumphantly.

The woman came from around the counter. "I only show the quality jewels to the most discerning of customers. And of course, to friends of Jao."

Leah pretended to hesitate, not wanting to be too obvious in her interest, but she definitely wanted to see the quality goods, and have a go at haggling down the price, no matter what was offered.

"All right," she agreed. "Though as I said, I'm just looking at the moment."

"Of course. I'll just lock up the store for a few minutes so we can take our time and not be disturbed." The woman moved toward the front door, sliding a bolt in place and turning the sign from *Open* to *Closed*.

Discomfited at first by the shopkeeper closing the store just for her, Leah supposed it made sense, since the shopkeeper couldn't very well leave the displays unattended while she took Leah in back. She must be assuming Leah was a rich American with plenty of American dollars to spend. Leah would look, but she'd made no promises to buy.

The woman gestured toward an entrance that was hung with strings of bright glass beads in lieu of a proper door and moved in that direction. Leah followed her through the beads into a tiny room that contained a round wooden table with two chairs and a small kitchen area with a stove and half-size refrigerator.

"Please." The woman gestured toward the table. "Have a seat, won't you? I will give you some iced coffee. Then I will bring out the trays of our finest jewels for your personal inspection."

"Thank you," Leah said. She took a seat at the table as the woman moved toward the kitchen and opened the refrigerator, removing a large glass pitcher with what looked like dark coffee inside it, along with a small white bottle Leah assumed was cream. The woman took a glass from the cabinet and filled it with the dark coffee and cream, stirring it into a caramel swirl.

As she watched the woman prepare the coffee, Leah realized she was in fact parched, and a nice glass of strong, sweet Thai iced coffee sounded pretty darn good at that moment, even if she was just being buttered up so she'd make a purchase.

The glass was set before her, along with a dish of saltine crackers. "To your health," the woman said. Leah picked up the glass and sipped. It was very sweet, too sweet, really, for Leah's taste, but it was cold and wet, and she was thirsty, so she took a long, deep gulp.

Oddly, she felt thirstier than she had a moment before, and there was a metallic taste in the back of her throat. She lifted the glass again, taking another gulp of the thick, sweet liquid to wash it away.

The woman smiled, nodding approvingly. "I'll bring the jewels. You drink that all up like a good girl."

Leah set the glass down harder than she'd meant to, clunking it against the scarred wood of the table. Her head felt suddenly heavy, her eyelids drooping down as if lead weights were attached to them. The sounds of the traffic outside the shop were muffled and there was a strange whooshing sound in her ears, as if her head were suddenly inside a seashell.

Leah tried to lift her hand to her face, but only succeeded in knocking over the glass, spilling the remaining liquid onto the table. "Help me. Something is wrong," she tried to say, but only managed a garbled, "Heh muh, sutha gah…"

The last thing she saw before her head hit the table was the shopkeeper, who reentered the room with two men holding coils of rope in their hands.

~*~

Leah awoke with a start, jerking violently out of a bad dream. She tried to push away the hair falling into her face, but found she couldn't move. She was lying on her side in a dark, hot room. Her hands were bound behind her back and her ankles were secured as well. She realized she was naked.

"Oh my god," she whispered, terror falling over her like a shroud. "What the hell happened? Where am I?"

She struggled to sit up, jerking hard at her restraints. She was bound with rope, thick and scratchy against her skin. Her head was pounding as she tried to lift it from the hard cot on which she lay.

"Help!" she cried out. "Someone help me!"

This couldn't be happening. How had she gotten here? She tried to think. Her mind felt sluggish, as if suspended in gelatin. *Think… what happened?* She'd been at the jewelry shop. She'd had some iced coffee while waiting for the shopkeeper…

She'd been kidnapped!

That coffee had tasted strange, now that she thought about it, but she'd been thirsty. Damn it! She'd been drugged and then kidnapped. To what purpose? Were they going to contact her family and ask for ransom? They had her clothing—they must have her purse too, including her passport and her driver's license.

How in god's name had this happened to her? She was careful! She had an instinct for people. How had the shopkeeper slipped past her radar? She'd traveled the world several times over, and never had anything like this happened. Even when she'd been in China and had her backpack stolen along with her passport, she'd handled things and found her way out of trouble.

Don't panic. Stay calm. You'll figure a way out of this, too. You aren't dead, so that's the first thing. They want something from you. Find out what it is and negotiate. You're Leah Jacobs. You can get out of this. You will *get out of this.*

She lay still for a long while, feeling the sweat trickling down her body as she counted slowly to one hundred, letting her mind clear. She did this several times until her heart had stopped thudding and her breathing had returned to something close to normal.

She decided to try again. "Hello?" she called, louder this time. "Is there someone there? Can you please untie me? Hello?"

The door opened, a slice of light momentarily blinding her. As Leah squinted against the light she saw two figures standing in the door. A bulb hanging from a string in the ceiling was flicked on, and as her eyes adjusted, she saw two men. One was tall with a darkly tan skin and thick, dark hair slicked back from his forehead. He wore a black tank top and black cargo pants tucked into army boots. The other man was much shorter, with straight black hair and Asian features. He wore a red T-shirt and jeans, flip flops on his feet. Both men looked to be in their mid to late twenties.

"You are American?" asked the Thai man in unaccented English.

"Please, what's going on? Untie me. Give me my clothes."

"You answer the question and only the question!" boomed the other man in what Leah recognized as a Russian accent. He took a step toward her, his hands clenched into fists, a scowl on his face.

"Y-yes," Leah sputtered, frightened. "Yes, I'm American." Thinking fast, she added, "My embassy knows I'm here in Pattaya. You'd better let me go right away or there's going to be trouble."

"Trouble?" The Thai man approached her with a leering grin. "You are the one in trouble, pretty lady. A nice American girl with *real* blond hair." He stared at her crotch. "We're going to sell you for a fortune."

"Sell me?" Leah struggled harder against the rough rope around her wrists. "Let me go! Let me go!" Her voice rose in a panicked squeal.

All at once both men were on her. The Thai guy rolled her onto her back, crushing her arms painfully beneath her body while the Russian grabbed her by the throat and squeezed until her cries trailed off to a muted, terrified whimper.

"You shut up!" he growled. "You want I hit you? You belong to us now and there's no damn thing you can do about it. You cost us lot of money, and you're going to earn that back, understand?"

Leah stared at him, mute with terror. Slowly he loosened his grip on her throat, a small mean smile moving over his face. "Listen good, girly. You lucky. Because you American and you blond, there are men willing to pay a lot for your ass. We could just whore you out, but we have something better in mind for you."

The Thai man nodded. "American girls need lots of training. You are not properly submissive like our women. Where we're taking you, you'll soon get rid of your stupid American ideas. You'll learn what it is to submit, and to properly please a man, no matter *what* they want of you. You'll learn, like the Thai girls, to do it all with a smile."

"Please," Leah finally managed to gasp. "This can't be happening. Please let me go."

Ignoring her, the Thai man pulled Leah back to her side and leaned over her, untying the knots at her ankles. "Please," she tried again, "I can get you money, if that's what you're after. Lots of money. Just give me clothes and my things—"

She was stunned into silence by the Russian, who slapped her cheek with his open palm, catching her ear at the same time and making it ring.

"Another word and I beat you with my fists!" The Russian raised his beefy hands and glared at her, his mouth twisted in an ugly sneer.

"Better to be quiet," the Thai man added, the smile on his face almost scarier than the other man's overt anger. "Women should be seen and not heard. Now spread your legs like a good girl. I want to check out that cunt of yours."

The Russian pressed hard against Leah's shoulders, holding her still against the canvas cot while the Thai forced her thighs apart. Her bound hands beneath her body caused her pelvis to thrust forward, as if she were offering herself. Leah squeezed her eyes shut, fear making her pant as rough fingers pushed inside her.

"Her cunt is nice and tight. Leah felt a savage twist on her right nipple. The Thai man laughed harshly. "Great tits, and they're real." She felt the man's finger rimming her asshole. "I'll bet she's never been fucked in the ass. Jao certainly steered us right on this one. It's our lucky day, Boris, my friend."

Boris' heavy hands relaxed against her shoulders and Leah twisted suddenly, rolling herself from the cot onto the ground, her only thought to escape. Her actions were chemical, bypassing the brain, the fight-or-flight adrenaline kicking in. Using her head as a battering ram, she launched herself against the legs of the smaller man, who fell back with a startled cry.

Somehow she got herself to her feet and lurched toward the closed door, though she realized as she stumbled forward, hands still tied behind her back, that she had no idea how the hell she was going to get it open. As she reached the door, strong arms wrapped around her torso, pulling her back and lifting her off the ground.

Her breath was knocked from her body as she was slammed facedown against the hard cot. "Fucking little *suka*!" the Russian roared. Sitting beside her, he grabbed her legs, roughly retying the rope around her ankles.

The Thai laughed cruelly. "She's a feisty one. What did I tell you? American girls are like wild animals. I don't have the patience for them myself, but Khalil will take good care of her. He'll pay top dollar, too. You know his fetish for blonds."

Leah was gasping like a fish, still trying to draw the air back into her tortured lungs, when she felt herself being lifted. She was flung like a sack of laundry over the Russian's large shoulder, her face against his muscular back. She could smell the acrid odor of his sweat, mingled with a heavy-scented aftershave.

They left the small room, entering a narrow alley. Though she had no idea if anyone would hear her, Leah began to scream. "Help me! I'm being kidnapped!"

She heard the pop of a car trunk and all at once she was dumped into the space, her shoulder making painful contact with the floor of the trunk. The lid slammed down over her, plunging her into darkness. Pulling futilely against the rope binding her wrists, Leah cried, "Let me out! Let me out!"

Car doors slammed and the engine started. Leah felt the car jerking forward, the tires squealing beneath her. As they moved along the streets, taking her who knew where, Leah tried desperately to slip her hands out of the rope cutting into her wrists. If only she could get herself free, she might find something in the trunk she could use as a weapon.

Leah felt each bump and pothole as the car moved along the busy streets, jerking to a stop at what Leah could only presume were traffic lights. She continued to call for help, but her voice seemed muted and tiny, trapped inside the trunk, obscured by the din of the traffic around her and the sound of the radio being played at top volume inside the car.

Something the Thai man had said had been niggling at her consciousness and now replayed itself in her mind. *Jao certainly steered us right on this one.* The concierge had set her up! His bullshit story and the brochure had been an elaborate ruse to get her into the back of that store. The woman was obviously in on it as well. The whole thing was some diabolical and well-orchestrated plot to kidnap innocent women!

After about twenty minutes, Leah felt the engine pick up speed and the road smoothed beneath them. Desperately she continued to work at the ropes, trying to reach the knots. They drove for a long time, it seemed to Leah, and she worked the whole time trying to free her hands. She had just managed to twist her right hand in a way that she could touch one of the knots with her fingers when the car lurched to a stop, causing her head to smack against a side of the trunk.

She heard the latch being released and then the trunk lid was lifted, letting sunlight and fresh air into the cramped space. "Please, let me go—" she began to cry, but she was cut off by the Thai man, who pushed her chin upward, forcing her to close her mouth, while the Russian bent down toward her and pressed a sticky piece of duct tape over her lips.

Silenced, Leah was lifted and again tossed over the Russian's big shoulder. She could smell the ocean on the air, which was cooler and breezier than it had been in the town, and in the near distance she could hear the sound of waves lapping against the shore.

They moved up a walkway flanked by well-tended green lawns. It struck Leah as odd that no one would notice or remark upon a naked, gagged and bound woman being carried over a man's shoulder in broad daylight.

Leah was taken up several broad stone steps. She heard what sounded like a door knocker falling heavily against wood—two quick taps, a pause and then another tap. This pattern was repeated a few times, and then the door opened.

Leah heard the murmur of male voices as she was brought into the building. Then someone said in English, "Welcome to my home, gentlemen. What have you procured for me today?" The man spoke with a British accent, though with the kind of precise pronunciation that made her think English wasn't the speaker's native language.

The Thai man answered, "As you can see, Mr. Khalil. Top quality American, pure blond, perfect body, lovely face. We know you've been looking for the perfect blond for a long time, Mr. Khalil. I think you'll find this one is exactly what you've been looking for."

"If I choose to take her, you'll get your due, don't worry. Where did you get her? Will she be missed?"

The Russian began walking again, carrying Leah along like a sack of potatoes. The Thai answered, "She was staying at the Pattaya Gold. Our operatives there scoped her out as a likely candidate. We did the usual background checks. She's traveling with a tour group, but the members come and go. We've already arranged for her to be checked out of the hotel, with all the usual precautions. It'll be a few days before anyone even notices she's gone."

Leah felt herself being lowered onto what turned out to be a couch. She was placed on her stomach, her hands still bound behind her. From where she lay, she saw the third man called Mr. Khalil. He appeared to be Middle Eastern, with olive skin, heavily-lashed dark eyes beneath thick brows, a long, hooked nose in a narrow face and wavy black hair. He was tall, his muscles lean and sculpted, putting Leah in mind of a professional ballet dancer. He was wearing a white silky dress shirt with several buttons opened, tucked into white pants of the same silky material. His feet were bare. He was strikingly handsome, and in other circumstances Leah would have been attracted. Now she was merely terrified.

"You did well, gentlemen. She is indeed a beauty. Such deep blue eyes, the color of the finest sapphires. And her hair, pure as spun gold." His eyes moving hungrily over her, Khalil said, "Untie her hands and flip her over. I want to see the rest of her body."

The Russian bent over Leah, tugging at the knots at her wrists. When her hands were free, he shoved roughly at her shoulder, forcing her onto her back. Leah instinctively tried to cover her naked body with her arms, but was stopped by the Thai man's barking command. "Hands at your sides! Do not attempt to cover yourself. You are being inspected."

With the three men towering over her, Leah had no choice but to obey. She let her arms flop weakly to her sides. Crouching beside her, Khalil drew his finger down Leah's cheek, moving it along her throat and down to her left breast. He cupped the breast in his large hand and nodded, his eyes hooding as his tongue moved over his lips. "Lovely," he murmured.

Leah wanted to spit in his handsome face and might have done so if her mouth hadn't been taped shut.

Letting her go, Khalil turned again to the abductors. "It is a shame you had to cover her mouth with that ugly tape. It is the mouth that indicates the sensuality, the potential for passion. I must see her mouth to judge properly if she is worthy of me." He shook his head, making a tsk'ing sound of regret. "Such a shame, but I understand the need to silence these willful American girls."

He leaned close, so close Leah felt his breath on her cheek. He smelled of cloves and peppermint, and when he smiled, he showed straight even teeth, perfectly white, but just beneath his smile was a wolf's leer. Leah closed her eyes and pressed herself into the sofa, desperately wishing she could vanish.

The man stroked her hair, his touch tender, as if they were lovers. "Do not be frightened, little one. You are only fulfilling your destiny. Woman is put on this earth to serve man. If I choose to so honor you, I will teach you to forget your harsh, abrasive American ways. You will no longer have to scrabble and scrape, forcing your way through the world as if you were a man. I will teach you the grace of a princess and the pure, elegant simplicity of a slave girl whose sole reason for being is to serve her master. Once I inspect your body for imperfections, and give you the chance to submit with humility and obedience to my dictates, you will be assessed to determine if you are worthy to become my slave."

Fuck you, you misogynistic asshole. I'll see you in hell first.

"If we take off the duct tape, do you promise to stay quiet, little one?" Khalil's tone was kind, his red lips curling into a smile, but Leah could sense the ruthlessness beneath the words.

Nevertheless, she nodded, desperate to have the sticky tape removed. Khalil touched her cheek with thumb and forefinger as he tugged at a corner of the tape. Leah closed her eyes, trying to steel herself to the anticipated pain as the tape was removed, but he was surprisingly gentle, pulling it slowly and carefully away from her mouth.

Once the duct tape was off, Leah took in a grateful breath of air through parted lips. "Please, you have to—" she began, but the man pressed two fingertips against her mouth, shaking his head.

"Not a word. My slaves do not speak unless spoken to. You must learn that immediately." His tone was hard, but it softened as he added, "Remember, little one. You *promised* to be quiet." He gazed into her eyes and she found herself staring back into his, mesmerized by their dark, liquid beauty, even as her brain tried to process his words.

My slaves.

The words ricocheted through Leah's brain. This was no dabbler in any sort of consensual BDSM scene. He was speaking literally, she realized with horror. This man *owned* other human beings.

Leah had heard of sex slave rings that kidnapped women, or tricked them into coming into the big city, having been told they were going to be given gainful employment, only to find out they had been conscripted into a prostitution ring.

But that sort of thing happened to gullible, innocent village girls in third world countries. It happened to young women with no say in their own lives or destinies, perhaps sold off by a family desperate for survival. It didn't happen to independent, experienced American women! It couldn't be happening now. Somehow, Leah had to stop this. She had to make them understand.

As soon as Khalil took his fingers from her mouth, she blurted, "There's been a terrible mistake!" She tried to bring authority to a voice she realized was shaking. "You can't do this. I demand to be returned to my hotel at once. My embassy will be making inquiries." She struggled against the rope still binding her wrists behind her back, painfully aware of how pathetic her appeal must seem.

Both the Russian and the Thai were grinning at her, but the Arab was not. His thick eyebrows furrowed over his dark, beautiful eyes. "You promised not to speak. You broke that promise." He pursed his lips and shook his head. "Broken promises," he said slowly in his careful English, "are met with harsh punishment."

He stepped back and clapped his hands. Two men of Asian descent appeared. Both were wearing silk pajama-like clothing like Khalil's, except theirs was all black. Though neither was especially tall, they were both well-muscled, with burly chests and thick necks and arms.

Glaring at Leah, Khalil said, "A beating and a night spent under the stairs will teach you to hold your tongue." To the guards he said, "Take her away!"

The guards' faces were like masks, devoid of any human emotion, as they moved to obey their master's orders. One man grabbed Leah's legs while the other slipped his hands beneath her shoulders. They swung her easily from the sofa and set off at a rapid pace, taking her from the opulent living room and down a long, narrow hallway. It happened so quickly she barely had time to react.

They hauled her through an open door into a room hung with ornate Oriental carpets on the walls, and also on the floor. There was a tall, thick post that went from floor to ceiling in the center of the room, with several lengths of chain hanging from its sides. The men set Leah down on her feet in front of the post.

Her trembling legs gave way and she sank to her knees. One man knelt behind her and, using a knife, cut away the ropes at her wrists and ankles. She was hauled again at once to her feet, her arms forcibly wrapped around the thick post and secured by the chains, which the men wound around her wrists to hold her in place.

"Please, please, I beg you, don't do this! Don't hurt me! Please, I can get you money. I can—"

Leah was stunned into silence by a sharp blow to her cheek though neither man said a word. Tears leapt to her eyes. One of the men pulled a dirty looking strip of white cotton from his pocket and forced it into Leah's mouth. The other wrapped a second strip around her head, holding the sour rag in place.

She couldn't see what they were doing behind her, but after a moment she felt the stinging blows of hard, knotted leather moving over her back. It wasn't like the sensual floggings she adored at the hands of her dominant lovers. There was no buildup, no pleasure mingling with erotic pain.

This was a beating, pure and simple, as they struck her over and over, methodically whipping her from shoulder to calf as she tried fruitlessly to avoid the blows. She felt herself nearly blacking out at one point, but the pain was too intense to let her slip away completely. She was revived by the fiery cut of the hard leather slapping relentlessly at her skin. She screamed again and again, but only a muffled mewling sound issued through the gag.

Finally the beating stopped, and the men released her arms from the whipping post. Again she collapsed to the carpet, this time falling over onto her side. As if she were an inanimate object, the men again picked her up between them and left the room, taking her again down the hall to a stairwell, beneath which was a small door secured by a padlock.

They set Leah, still gagged and nearly insensible with pain and terror, roughly on the ground. One of the men took a key from a long chain around his neck and used it to open the lock. The gag was pulled from her mouth, but before she could try once again to plead her case, the men thrust her roughly into the dark cupboard-like space beneath the stairs. Before she could react, the door was shut, plunging her into darkness.

Leah sat still for several hours, or maybe it was only minutes, too stunned and terrified to move. The back side of her body felt as if it had been flayed, the skin stripped from the muscle. She reached back, carefully touching the abraded flesh. It was tender to the touch, but at least the guards had obeyed the directive not to cut the skin.

She supposed she should be grateful at least that Khalil hadn't wanted them to beat her to a bloody pulp. Thank god for small favors. Very small favors, she thought bitterly, as she tried to make herself more comfortable on the hard floor in the dank, dark space to which she'd been confined. The air was damp and smelled of rotting wood and dust.

Blindly groping, Leah felt in the dark for the boundaries of the cupboard. The space was just wide enough for her to lie down. The ceiling was too low for standing, and even sitting, she had to bend her neck forward a little to keep from hitting her head. The walls were of rough, unfinished planks of wood. The floor was also of wood, and covered in a film of dirt or soot.

Something skittered lightly over her foot and Leah screamed, jerking her head back and banging it against the ceiling in the process. When her heart had finally slowed its hammering enough for her to breathe without gasping, she forced herself to calm down. *It was only a bug, and probably way more terrified of you than you were of it.* She took several long, deep breaths and counted slowly to ten over and over again.

When she was calm enough to think, her mind was suddenly teeming with questions. What was going to happen to her? How long were they going to leave her in this prison cell? Would she be left to die here?

Leah started to tremble again, but forced herself to be rational. *They aren't going to leave you to die. You're a commodity, to be sold. They can't sell a corpse.*

This line of thought didn't give her much comfort. Still, where there was life, there was hope, she told herself staunchly. But the really scary thing was, there wasn't a soul who knew where she was.

Devin. Come save me!

He'd left her that lovely note. What would he think when she didn't show up to meet him for dinner? Would he think she was just some fickle young American idiot who had stood him up?

No, surely he would realize something was wrong. After the amazing night they'd spent together, and the incredible promise of their time to come, he would know she'd have been there if she could. He would know something was very, very wrong.

Leah closed her eyes against the darkness, letting the image of Devin fill her mind's eye. "Please," she whispered aloud, "Find me, Devin. Rescue me from this nightmare."

Chapter 3

Devin drummed his fingers on the bar impatiently. Where was Leah? Though it was good to be finally closing the deal for some prime beachfront property for his firm, the last place he had wanted to be was in stuffy offices signing endless piles of paperwork, or politely sipping tea with Thai businessmen. Not when he'd had to leave a beautiful, naked woman in his bed.

He was glad he'd told her seven, though he'd hoped to escape sooner. As it was, he'd barely had time to shower and shave before racing down to the bar to meet Leah and, hopefully, pick up where they'd left off. He looked at his watch again. 7:16. Damn it, where was she? He'd have to give her a nice, hard spanking for being late.

The thought made him smile, and his cock nudged in his pants at the idea of putting her over his knee and swatting that luscious little bottom until it was cherry red. But then, she would like that, wouldn't she? Yes, of course she would, but that just made it all the sweeter.

"Hello, handsome. Waiting for someone?" A petite woman with long, dark glossy black hair and too much makeup on her teenage face sidled onto the stool beside him. She smiled coquettishly, thrusting her small, barely concealed breasts toward him. "I can make you very happy, please, sir. I am a good girl. I do anything you say."

Devin glanced at the young prostitute and shook his head. The sex trade was still huge business in Pattaya, despite the local government's effort to clean things up and create a more family-friendly image for the beach town.

"I'm sorry," Devin said to the smiling young woman who was now pressing her tiny breasts against his arm. He pulled his arm away. "I *am* waiting for someone."

The girl's smile vanished and she turned from him, moving down the bar toward another man hunched over his beer. Devin heard her chirp, "Hello, handsome. Waiting for someone?"

Devin reached for his beer and took a long pull. Why hadn't he gotten Leah's mobile number? Or even asked what room she was staying in? Truth was, he'd been so eager to tumble into bed with her, he had behaved like a teenager, thinking only in the moment.

Now he was stuck in this damn bar, and Leah was twenty minutes late.

Surely she hadn't changed her mind? Not after the amazing night they'd spent together? No. Something must have come up to detain her. He needed to chill. In a moment she'd come though the large doorway that led to the hotel's lobby, her golden hair flying, her cheeks kissed by the sun. Breathlessly she'd explain why she was late, and Devin knew he would forgive her instantly.

He turned toward the doorway, as if he could conjure her there by sheer will. After a minute he turned back, signaling to the bartender for another beer.

Damn it, Leah. Where are you?

Devin watched the group of tourists enter the bar. They were talking loudly in American accents as they settled in one of the booths and gestured for a waitress. Leah had mentioned she was traveling with a tour group. Taking a chance these were her companions, Devin rose and approached them.

It was now 8:00 and he was deeply worried. "Excuse me," he ventured. "I've been waiting for an American young lady by the name of Leah Jacobs. She was supposed to meet me at seven. I confess I'm rather worried about her. Would any of you happen to know her?"

A red-headed woman in her early thirties looked up at Devin. "Are you Devin Lyons?"

Hope flared in Devin's chest. "Why, yes. I take it you know Leah? Have you seen her today?"

"Yes, she's with our tour group. I saw her early this afternoon. She mentioned she'd met you. She was, uh, quite enthusiastic about you." The woman smiled knowingly. "She wouldn't go down to the beach with me. Said she had to go shopping for something new to wear for your dinner date." The woman frowned, looking around the bar as if Leah were hiding somewhere. "She's not here?"

"I wouldn't worry about it." A man in his forties, overweight with graying sandy-blond hair and the rosy complexion of a heavy drinker, smirked at Devin. "Leah's just a kid. No offense, buddy, but she probably found something better to do. A wild party, a chance to hang out with someone famous — coulda been anything with that one."

The redhead seemed to ponder this. "Hmm, it is possible, I suppose. Leah has been known to go off on her own for a day or two." She pursed her lips thoughtfully, her eyes moving appraisingly over Devin as she slowly shook her head. "Though Leah isn't one to kiss and tell, it was pretty obvious she couldn't wait to see you again. I don't see her not showing." She frowned and reached into her handbag, pulling out her mobile phone. "I'll just text her real quick. She's pretty good about texting back."

Devin nodded gratefully, glad someone at the table was taking him seriously. "Thanks. That would be great."

The other woman in the booth, a fifty-something buxom blond with too much makeup, smiled brightly at Devin and then waved her hand rather dismissively at the redhead. "Don't listen to her. Kara's just a worrywart. Leah will resurface eventually. She always does. By the way, I just *love* your accent." She scooted closer to the man beside her and patted the seat. "Why don't you join us? My name's Beth. That's Kara texting your would-be girlfriend. This here's Jack." She gestured toward the man she'd pushed closer to the wall. He was also in his fifties, Devin guessed, with salt and pepper hair and a prominent nose. She pointed at the smirking man beside Kara. "And that's Frank."

"Yeah, have a seat. Looks like you could use a refill." Frank lifted a pitcher of beer, using it to gesture toward the nearly empty beer mug in Devin's hand.

Devin hesitated. He didn't really feel like joining the Americans but they were his only link to Leah. "All right," he said. "Thank you."

He looked anxiously toward Kara, who was staring down at her phone. She met his eyes, shaking her head. "Nothing yet. Maybe they're right. She might be at a club or something. Let's give her a few minutes."

Devin nodded, but his earlier sense of foreboding increased. He waited another twenty minutes, answering the questions put forward by the Americans in a distracted way, asking Kara every few minutes if she'd heard back from Leah.

Eventually Kara put her hand over Devin's, her expression kind. "Look, I don't usually give out another woman's phone number, but I think Leah will forgive me this time."

She gave Devin Leah's number, which he punched into his mobile and saved in his contacts. "Leah's in the room next to mine—room 232. I'm sure we'll hear from her by morning," she added. "This is probably just Leah being Leah."

Thanking the Americans, Devin left the bar and went to the elevators. He got off at the second floor, scanning the numbers until he found Leah's door. He knocked and waited a few seconds, and then knocked again, louder this time. "Leah!" he called. "It's Devin. Please open the door."

Silence. He rattled the knob and then pulled out his card key, swiping it through the slot, though of course that did no good. He called her mobile, which went straight to an automated voicemail. He left a message, trying to keep the panic out of his voice. "Hey, Leah. It's Devin. I thought we had a date at seven. It's nearly nine. Call and let me know you're all right."

Returning to the lobby, he approached the check-in counter. A thin young Thai man smiled politely at him. "May I help you, sir?"

"Yes," Devin said tersely. "I need to speak with the occupant of room 232, Leah Jacobs. Could you ring the room please?"

"Certainly, sir." The man lifted a phone receiver and punched in a few numbers. He listened a few seconds, and then shook his head. "I am sorry, sir. There is no answer. Can I help you in some other way?"

Devin shoved his hands into his pockets and pondered what to do next. Should he just wait in his room for her to show up? What if the Americans were wrong and she was out there somewhere, lost or in trouble? She was a young woman alone in a strange country. He didn't care how savvy a traveler she claimed to be, it was a dangerous world out there. He couldn't just sit idly by while Leah might be in trouble.

Pulling his hands from his pockets, he pressed them flat against the counter. "Yes. You can direct me to nearest police station."

~*~

Leah awoke with a start. It took her several moments to realize where she was. She was lying on her left side, curled tightly into a fetal ball. Her shoulder ached from when they'd thrown her into the trunk and the skin on her back, ass and legs felt tender and sore.

Thirsty. Water. I need water. Leah's tongue felt thick and her lips were dry and chapped. There was still a bitter, metallic taste in the back of her throat, no doubt left over from the drugged coffee. She knew she should have been hungry—she'd had nothing since breakfast, which was who knew how long ago. But her stomach was bunched into a hard, cold knot, the anxiety filling her belly leaving no room for food.

As she lay there, her mind still fogged from fear and exhaustion, she became aware of her full bladder. She rolled carefully onto her back in an effort to ease the pressure. In her initial blind exploration of the cramped space she hadn't felt anything like a toilet, or even a bucket placed there for the purpose. What did they expect her to do?

When she couldn't take the ache in her bladder any longer, she forced herself to her hands and knees and began moving carefully over the dusty, hard flooring. Her hand closed over a bit of fabric, and she realized they must have tossed the makeshift gag in with her. She kept it as she moved slowly along the floorboards.

Based on the padlock on the small door, and Khalil's command to put her under the stairs, Leah surmised she wasn't the first woman to be imprisoned in this cupboard. Other poor women had probably spent time here, and probably had to pee. What had they done?

Leah had squatted over her share of holes in the ground in her travels. She moved her hands in light, sweeping arcs over the floor, looking for a crack big enough to use as a latrine. In one of the corners she found what she'd been looking for—an actual hole in the planks, a circle probably cut for the purpose. If it wasn't meant for that, too damn bad—she was going to explode if she didn't pee.

Positioning herself carefully in the dark, she squatted over the hole, sighing with relief as she emptied her bladder. Using the gag, she wiped herself as best she could, and then left the soiled cotton about a foot away from the makeshift latrine.

She moved to the far side of the space and again lay down on her side, her mind racing. The first thing she had to do was get out of this little space. She thought about crawling over to the door and banging. She could beg to be let out, but she knew even as she thought about this that it would do no good.

That crazy Arab bastard had some kind of god complex, and apparently those he kept around him shared the view, or at least were paid enough to pretend to. He had those henchmen to do his bidding, and he'd been very clear about his *slave girls* not speaking out of turn. That's what had landed her in this prison under the stairs in the first place. She wouldn't compound her troubles by doing it again. She'd stay quiet, biding her time while she figured out what to do next.

For the first time since she'd taken her leave of absence from law school the year before, she wished she'd listened to her parents and stayed put in the States, finishing her degree. Instead of finding herself naked and locked in some madman's home in Thailand, she could be surrounded by a pile of books in a nice, safe library, pouring over tort law and case studies.

When her grandmother had died two years before, Leah had been as surprised as anyone to discover the old woman had owned a life insurance policy for $750,000, every penny of which she had bequeathed to Leah, her only grandchild.

"Life's short, baby," she used to say to Leah. "See the world! Take risks, experience life. People grow old too fast. Live a little!" Leah's grandmother didn't share her parents' view that adulthood meant buckling down and earning a living. Leah's uncles had no children, so Leah had been her grandmother's favorite by default.

An oft-repeated motto of her grandmother's had been: *Life is short – eat dessert first*. When she'd died at the age of eighty-two, at least she'd had plenty of dessert, Leah thought with a sad smile.

Leah's grandfather, by contrast, had been a dour man who didn't like to travel to the next state, much less another country. He'd died of a massive heart attack when Leah was fifteen. Her grandmother had begun to travel only after his death. She had taken Leah on trips to Europe and Asia on several occasions, awakening in Leah the same wanderlust, which had apparently skipped a generation.

Her grandmother hadn't been able to travel since her stroke, but continued to encourage Leah to do so on her own. Leah had done some volunteer work in Nepal and Nigeria in the summer before law school, but "real life", as her parents called it, had intervened, putting her dreams of continued world travel on a backburner. When she found herself suddenly with a fortune at her command, she'd decided to take a breather and take her grandmother's advice.

Truth to tell, though she hadn't admitted it to her parents, who were both attorneys themselves and dead set on Leah following in their footsteps, she had hated law school, every mind numbing, boring second of it. She'd chosen environmental law as her career goal, thinking this sounded sexier and more socially redeeming than the corporate law both her parents practiced. She was still forced to sit through seminars and lectures in which she would suddenly be called on to hold forth on some esoteric topic, pretending she knew what she was talking about and praying she wasn't making a total ass out of herself. She spent every night slogging through endless case studies, trying to stay awake and figure out the salient points, or cramming for exams.

As she'd traveled these past eighteen months, the thought of returning to law school had receded further and further from her mind. Though she'd had no idea what else she wanted to do, at least her sudden windfall no longer made what she was going to do with the rest of her life such a pressing issue.

And now that choice had been stolen from her. Her life might well be over. At least the life she'd known.

Leah's ears pricked at the sound of muffled voices on the other side of the cupboard door. After a moment, the door was pulled open, letting light into the space. Leah, who had been dozing fitfully, came wide awake. She rolled to a sitting position, drawing up her legs and crossing her arms over them.

"The master is ready to see you."

Chapter 4

The same two thugs who had manhandled her earlier were standing just outside the cupboard door. Leah had no idea how long she'd been held beneath the stairs. It felt like an eternity. Even though she was terrified at what the man they called master wanted from her, she was desperate to get out of the dank, musty enclosure. Even more, she was desperate for something to drink.

On her hands and knees, she crawled out of the space. Though acutely aware of her nudity, she started to stand, but was pushed roughly down by one of the men. "Master says you crawl. Master says untrained American girls are no better than dogs."

Leah felt her face heat at these words, but she didn't try to rise again. The men sandwiched her, one in front, the other behind, as she began to crawl along the gleaming hardwood hallway. She was led back into the large main room of the house, to a broad, curving set of thickly carpeted stairs.

The men forced her to stay on her hands and knees as she climbed the stairs. Her muscles felt like jelly, her arms actually shaking as they supported her weight. It seemed to take forever to get up those stairs, but once at the top, one of men stopped her with a touch to her shoulder.

"Wait," he said.

The other moved toward a set of large doors made of rich, dark mahogany and knocked softly. Leah heard a deep voice say, "Enter," from behind the doors. The man opened both the doors and turned back to the other henchman, who reached down, giving Leah a smack on the ass, indicating she was to move.

Humiliated and frightened in equal measure, Leah crawled into the room. It was a bedroom, though as large as her entire apartment back in the States. There was a huge bed over which hung a canopy of flowing, dove gray silk embroidered with hundreds of what looked like diamonds, sparkling in the early morning sun that poured through huge, floor-to-ceiling windows, beyond which she could see the ocean.

So she'd been left to spend the night in that wretched cupboard, while this bastard slept peacefully in his sumptuous room. Khalil wasn't in the bed at the moment, but was sitting at a round table covered in a white linen tablecloth, a bowl of fresh cut fruit, a crystal goblet filled with what looked like water and a silver pot of coffee in front of him. There was a second, empty chair across from him.

Khalil was wearing a black silk robe and his dark hair was wet as if he'd just come from a shower. Leah would have killed for a shower at that moment. Not to mention some of that fresh fruit and some water, please, some water.

Khalil stared down at her, lifting an eyebrow. "Ah, the golden American beauty. Have you learned your lesson, little one?"

Not entirely sure what the lesson had been — most of yesterday's events were shrouded in a fog of terror and pain — Leah said anyway, "Yes, sir."

Lifting his chin, Khalil waved toward the two men, who bowed in unison and left the room, closing the doors behind them. Turning back to Leah, he smiled, baring his perfect, white teeth. "Come," he said. "Sit here beside me." He gestured toward a small, flat pillow on the floor by his feet.

Leah would have much rather been invited to sit in the chair across from him. She wanted to swipe the glass of water and chug it down, and then grab the fresh fruit with both hands and stuff it into her mouth. At the sight and smell of the fruit, her stomach had come awake with a vengeance.

Still, kneeling was better than crouching like an animal on her hands and knees, her bare breasts swaying. She crawled to the pillow and set her bottom down on it, drawing her legs up in an effort to hide some of her nakedness.

Khalil shook his head. "No, no, do not cover yourself. A slave girl never covers herself. It is a sign of great disrespect."

Fuck you, you dirty, filthy, nasty bastard. Hoping her face remained neutral, Leah forced her legs to unfold. She felt herself blushing as Khalil eyed her body, his dark eyes glittering.

"Much better." Turning back to the table, Khalil lifted a tiny coffee cup and took a sip. "I trust the beating you received and the one night under the stairs will be sufficient to remind you that slaves only speak when spoken to. Or more to the point, only when asked a direct question."

He selected a piece of pineapple and placed it in his mouth. He chewed slowly while Leah salivated. "As to how you must address me going forward, sir is a gesture of respect, but it's not enough for a mere slave. You will call me Master. Understand?"

For the first time since she'd been captured, fury overcame terror. She felt her mouth turning down into a frown, despite her effort to keep her expression neutral. Khalil picked up the glass of clear, lovely water and tilted it to his lips, taking a long drink. Setting down the glass, he chose a plump, red strawberry from the bowl of fruit and popped it into his mouth.

Leah nearly whimpered with need.

Play the game. They're just words. You won't be able to escape if you end up dying of thirst.

Forcing herself to speak, Leah managed, "Yes, Master."

Khalil nodded, as if he were a king accepting his due. Who the hell was this man?

"Are you thirsty, slave?"

Again the fury threatened to bubble over at his degrading appellation. Leah was nobody's slave! But thirst won out over pride. Leah nodded, even managing to add, "Yes, please, Master."

She watched as he lifted the glass of water and handed it down to her. A brief and sudden fantasy of throwing the water in his face and then breaking the glass over his head flashed through her mind, but Leah knew she had no chance against this strong, well rested and well fed man, not to mention two thugs who were probably waiting just outside the door.

She drank what was left of the water, quickly draining the glass.

"More?" Khalil asked, lifting the crystal water pitcher.

"Yes, please…Master," Leah forced herself to say. If Khalil noticed that her hand was trembling as she held up the glass to be refilled, he didn't remark upon it. Once it was full, she drank again, the pure, cool water flooding her parched mouth and throat.

"Care for some fruit, little one?" Khalil plucked a raspberry from the bowl and held it out between thumb and forefinger. Leah noticed the thick gold ring he wore on his index finger. His nails were manicured and buffed to a shine.

She reached for the tiny piece of fruit, but Khalil shook his head. "I'll feed you. It amuses me to do so."

Leah opened her mouth, silently congratulating herself on not trying to strangle the bastard. Food was more important than dignity right now. She chewed the delicious berry, watching hungrily as he selected a chunk of banana. He continued to feed her several more pieces of fruit, the net result of which was, her appetite now thoroughly whetted, she was hungrier than ever.

But instead of offering her something of more substance, Khalil lifted a thick linen napkin and daubed at the corners of her mouth as if she were an infant. "That's enough for now. You shall have a meal later this morning, once you are showered and properly groomed."

Before she could stop herself, Leah began to plead, "Please, sir, uh, Master. You can't keep me like this. There's been some terrible mistake. I'm an American citizen."

"Not another word!" Khalil boomed. He was glowering down at her, fury moving like a storm over his face. "Foolish, evil girl! You said you had learned your lesson! Now you go on babbling as if you had a right to speak! You have no rights! You exist now solely for *my* pleasure."

He took a breath and ran his hands down his chest, as if trying to regain his composure. Speaking in a quieter voice, he continued, "And just so you understand once and for all, little one, there has been no mistake. I paid a very high price for you, my blond beauty, and the sooner you reconcile yourself to your fate, the better off you'll be."

He lifted a small bell from the table and rang it. The doors to the bedroom opened at once and the two men came striding in. They stopped a respectful distance away, their thickly muscled arms crossed over their chests.

"Take her away," Khalil said imperiously. "It is clear the girl requires further punishment. Beat her, muzzle her and take her to the kennels."

Leah was again dragged to the room with the whipping post. As before, the two men forced her to stand against the post and wrap her arms around it so they could chain her in place.

Again she felt the stinging bite of knotted leather against skin still tender from the first beating. They whipped her back and ass until she was sagging against the post, the weight of her body supported solely by the chains around her wrists.

When they let her go she slumped to the ground. She was covered in sweat, which stung along her back and sides. Her face was streaked with tears and snot. The only sound in the room was her whimpering cries — both men remained silent and stoic-faced, seemingly indifferent to her suffering.

One of them used a bandana to wipe her face, none too gently. The other produced a sort of leather harness with straps attached. The two men knelt on either side of Leah, one pinning her arms behind her back while the other strapped the contraption over her mouth and jaw. This, she realized with horror, was the muzzle that bastard Khalil had referred to. The leather that covered the lower half of her face was soft, but completely confining. Once the thug was done buckling the muzzle behind her head, Leah could still breathe through her nose, but her jaw was locked shut.

The men stood and the stockier of the two flipped Leah over his shoulder, carrying her as the Russian had done. They passed along the hallway and down the stairs. Leah heard voices as they made their way to the front door. Though she couldn't see much from her uncomfortable vantage point, she was vaguely aware of people sitting and standing in the large room. Shock and fear, along with physical pain from the whipping, prevented her from taking in much of the scene.

They passed through other rooms and arrived at a door that opened to the outside. Leah could hear the sound of barking dogs in the near distance as they moved through some kind of courtyard in the warm morning air. When they passed through the gate of a chain link fence the barking grew louder, mingling with excited yelps and whining.

All at once, a pack of dogs surrounded them, bared, pointed teeth and snarling lips in Leah's line of vision. Her heart felt like it was going to explode out of her chest. Were these monsters going to leave her here to be torn to shreds by a pack of rabid dogs? She realized she was screaming with terror, but her cries were muted by the muzzle.

The man set her down on her bottom in the dirt, and the dogs closed in around her, sniffing and growling. "Wait! Help! Don't leave me here!" Leah tried to cry, but her jaws were clamped shut by the leather.

The gate clanked shut behind the men and Leah was left alone, naked and defenseless amidst a pack of vicious dogs. Curling in on herself, she hid her head in her arms, her muscles rigid with terror as the dogs closed in around her. She tried to gird herself for what she knew was coming, praying it didn't last too long. But instead of sharp teeth ripping through her flesh, she felt the slobbery wet kiss of a dog tongue moving over her cheek.

Jerking her head back, Leah opened her eyes. She was nose to snout with a handsome German Shepherd with soulful brown eyes. To Leah's stunned relief, the dog gave a happy bark and began to wag her tail.

Another dog, a sleek black hound of some kind, nosed between Leah's legs, sniffing at her crotch. Leah, sitting in a patch of damp dirt, realized with dismay she must have wet herself in her fear. Scooting away from the curious animal, Leah closed her legs. She felt weak with relief to realize these dogs were friendly, and not the rabid killers she had feared. Tentatively she held her hands, palms down, for the dogs to sniff. There were eight of them altogether, all large animals who appeared to be in their prime.

Pushing herself to her feet, Leah stood tall over the pack, wishing she could speak to them. She looked all around the area, searching out any possible guards. Seeing no one, she reached behind her head, hoping to unbuckle the harness. She was unable to get it off, however, as a small padlock had been secured through the buckle, rendering it impossible to remove.

At least she wasn't bound hand and foot. She was free to move around the kennel, which was really more of a large, fenced-in dirt yard. There was a large water trough in one corner, with eight empty metal food bowls nearby. There were various dog bones and toys scattered around the area, and a tin roof extended out over one corner of the space, offering shade. On the dirt beneath the tin canopy stood what looked like a long, low trampoline.

Leah walked toward the trampoline, the dogs keeping her company every step of the way. Upon closer inspection, she realized it was a kind of large outdoor dog bed. To prove the point, several of the dogs climbed aboard and curled into nap position, heads on their paws, tongues lolling in the mid morning heat.

Leah moved toward the water trough. She would have been more than willing to drink from it, but the muzzle precluded that opportunity. At least she could wash up a little. Reaching into the trough, she splashed handfuls of the cool water over her body, trying to clean herself as best she could. Several of the dogs jumped excitedly around her, trying to bite at the splashing water. A couple of them nosed empty tin bowls and looked back at her beseechingly.

Though the circumstance was surreal in the extreme, Leah felt, for the first time since the nightmare had begun in the jewelry shop, a little of the fear lift from her heart. The pure, innocent, doggy happiness of the animals cavorting around her actually made her smile beneath the leather mask.

Some of the dirt and sweat removed, Leah made her way around the perimeter of the high chain link fence. The top of the fence was covered in coils of barbed wire, the gate locked from the outside. She could see the ocean in the distance, and off to the left she saw a startling sight. There were half a dozen horses visible through some trees. They were frozen in place, some in mid gallop, some gazing regally toward the horizon, one rearing back on its hind legs. It took her brain a moment to process that these were not real horses, but statues sculpted from some kind of smooth white stone.

She was distracted from the curious sight by movement in her peripheral vision. Turning back toward the villa, Leah saw two men in the distance wearing coveralls, bending over flowerbeds.

They were either unaware of her or indifferent to her presence. Briefly Leah considered trying to attract their attention, but thought better of it. No doubt she'd been carried right past them and they hadn't lifted a finger in her defense. They were probably well-paid to do their jobs and keep their mouths shut.

The sun was higher in the sky now, the air humid. Leah was bone-weary. She looked around the fenced-in pen, her eyes resting on the trampoline where several of the dogs had already settled down for their morning nap. Would they let a human join them?

Tentatively, Leah made her way to the trampoline and sat cautiously on the edge. The dogs already there lifted their heads, but made no move or growl to warn her away. Two more dogs climbed aboard and moved in circles over the canvas, finally settling. Leah inched herself fully onto the trampoline. She sat between two of the dogs, stroking their heads. One of them, a pit bull with a perennial doggy grin, lifted his head and lay it down on her bare thigh, closing his eyes in apparent ecstasy as she scratched him behind the ears.

Leah didn't want to lie down amidst the animals, aware from growing up with two dogs that it was better to keep her height advantage so they would continue to regard her as the alpha. So instead she scooted between the animals until her back was against the fence. She leaned carefully against the chain links, her skin still raw from the whipping. Drawing her knees up, she rested her head against them, wrapping her arms around her legs. It wasn't the most comfortable position, but at least she was out in the fresh air, and the dogs were far friendlier than anyone else she had encountered in this nightmarish establishment.

Closing her eyes, somehow she slept.

Chapter 5

Leah awoke with a start as the dogs leaped suddenly from the trampoline, barking excitedly. A man she hadn't seen before entered the kennel with two large buckets in his hands. The dogs raced to the empty food bowls, tails wagging furiously.

The man moved toward the bowls, pushing through the excited canine throng. All at once he noticed Leah, who was huddled on the trampoline, adrenaline pumping through her limbs, though she remained still as a cornered animal.

He looked startled at first. Embarrassment and pity moved over his features, and the tight fear that had gripped Leah's heart at his appearance eased somewhat. He said something to her in Thai, his tone sympathetic, though she didn't understand a word. She, of course, couldn't reply, muzzled as she was by the leather harness. Shaking his head, the man turned away, focusing on his task of feeding the animals. When he was done, the dogs eagerly and noisily wolfing down their breakfasts, he turned to her again, shaking his head, sympathy etched in his features. This time she recognized two of his words from her travel guide knowledge of Thai. They were spoken softly.

"I'm sorry."

He wasn't so sorry that he did anything to help her, however. Turning his back, he left the yard, locking the gate behind him.

Perhaps an hour had passed. Leah was sitting on the edge of the trampoline, several dogs once again curled contentedly around her. All at once, the dogs lifted their heads, looking toward the gate. Several of them leaped from the bed and raced toward the fence, barking excitedly. Lean saw the two guards who had beaten and then dumped her in the kennel approaching.

She stiffened, her heart jumpstarting into a pounding beat as she watched them unlock the gate and enter the kennel. The German Shepherd had remained with Leah. Perhaps sensing her anxiety, the dog growled softly as the men came near.

"Come," the shorter of the two men said, gesturing toward Leah.

Leah slid from the low trampoline and stood, wrapping her arms around her bare torso. She was almost sorry to leave the dogs—at least she'd been safe among them. And who knew what new horror awaited her?

~*~

Devin approached the front desk. The woman behind the check-in counter looked up. "Yes, sir?" She smiled pleasantly.

He'd tried to file a missing persons complaint with the police, but they'd refused to lift a bloody finger, saying it wasn't their job to keep tabs on tourists who went missing for a few hours, and blandly suggesting he check back in the morning if she still hadn't appeared. He'd spent a nearly sleepless night pacing his hotel room, calling her mobile repeatedly, with no results.

He must have finally fallen asleep at some point, because he awoke to the sound of the alarm blaring at seven. After a quick shower to wake himself, he rushed down to the lobby, this time determined to get results.

"I need to connect with one of the guests," Devin said firmly. "Her name is Leah Jacobs. She is checked in to room 232 but I'm afraid she might be missing. Please call the room for me at once." He'd already decided to insist they take him up to the room and open the door, so he could see for himself she wasn't in there. He drummed the counter anxiously while he waited for the woman behind the counter to pull up the information on her computer.

After a moment she looked up with the ubiquitous Thai polite smile. "I'm sorry. We have no one by that name registered at the hotel."

"What?" Devin frowned, his stomach clutching. "She was here as of yesterday. I'm certain of it. Look again. It's Jacobs. Leah Jacobs." He spelled the name, trying to keep his patience in check.

The woman tapped again on her keyboard, staring at her monitor. "That is correct, sir. She checked out yesterday morning."

"No, she didn't," Devin contradicted. "Her group isn't scheduled to leave until today. You've made a mistake."

"Excuse me, is there a problem?" A Thai man dressed in a shiny silk suit, his dark hair slicked back from his forehead, appeared beside Devin. The gold metal tag pinned over his breast pocket read *Concierge*.

"Yes. There's a group of Americans traveling together. Leah Jacobs, a part of the group, is staying in room 232. Ms.—" Devin glanced at the woman's name tag, hoping he was pronouncing it correctly, "Jetirawat is telling me she checked out."

"Ah, yes. I know the lady. Blond hair, blue eyes, early twenties. She checked out yesterday morning. I personally handled her checkout. She was heading on to…" The man squinted at the ceiling, as if trying to recall a conversation. "Ah, yes. She told me she was heading to Bangkok."

Devin shook his head. What the hell was going on here?"Look, I was with the lady yesterday morning. We made plans to meet again last night. There is no way she checked out. You're just plain wrong." Devin realized he was clenching his fists. His heart felt as if someone were squeezing it.

The concierge offered a bland, sympathetic smile. "Ah, pretty girl, so young, eh? These Americans, they do what they like." His smile curved into something more knowing, his eyebrows lifting with supposed understanding. Devin wanted to sock him in the jaw. "Forget about that silly American girl," the man continued. "There are so many lovely ladies here in Pattaya for you to choose from. I can recommend some excellent clubs—"

"There was nothing silly about her," Devin snapped, furious at the man's presumption and rudeness. "And I'm not interested in random young women. I'm looking for Leah Jacobs. Don't you understand? She might in trouble. How dare you talk to me like that!"

The concierge shrugged his shoulders, lifting his hands in a gesture of surrender. "I beg your pardon if I offended, but what can I tell you, sir? The girl is gone. Long gone."

~*~

The men flanked her on either side, each taking hold of an upper arm as they propelled her from the kennel. She was desperately thirsty and would have begged the men for water if she hadn't been gagged.

They led her back into the large house, though this time, instead of taking her back into the main room, they took her up a narrow staircase just inside the back door. When they reached the top of the stairs, Leah was terrified she was going to be beaten again and thrust into another cupboard, but instead she was led into a large, sumptuous bathroom.

The floors and walls were tiled in white marble shot through with strands of silver, gold and green. There was a huge sunken tub that took up one side of the room. It was filled with water, a fragrant steam rising from the surface. Leah's skin, covered in dirt, dried sweat and dog hair, itched with longing.

She was directed to a toilet set discreetly behind a screen. She sat, embarrassed to go in front of these thugs, but aware she'd better seize the opportunity. When she was done, they led her back into the main bathroom.

"Kneel." The taller man pointed to a thick bath rug beside the tub and Leah sank gratefully to her feet on the soft pile, staring longingly at the bath. To her relieved delight, the man unlocked and unbuckled the leather harness, removing it from her head.

Leah touched her jaw, which was wet with sweat and aching with disuse. She opened her mouth carefully, reveling in the freedom to do so after so many hours.

"Drink." The guard handed her a glass of water. Leah took the glass and gratefully drained it.

"Get into the tub, filthy girl. Alex will take care of you." The shorter guard was pointing to the bathtub. If she was filthy, he and his thug partner were certainly to blame, but Leah held her tongue. Gingerly she climbed into the water. It was hot, but not too hot, and moved like silky heaven over her skin as she lowered herself down.

The taller man went to a counter and lifted a small brass bell. Its tinkle echoed against the marble walls and within a few seconds a tall solid-looking man with long, lank brown hair pulled back into a ponytail entered the room. Leah presumed this was the Alex the guard had referred to. He was wearing a dark blue robe that resembled a kimono, his feet bare. He wore what looked to Leah like a slave collar made of silver metal around his neck, a large O ring at its center. There were matching cuffs around his wrists and ankles.

The guard who had rung the bell pointed toward Leah. "She's to have a full grooming. She is to be presented to the harem steward for inspection."

Harem steward! Did harems actually still exist? Weren't they the province of the Middle East, not the Far East? But then, Khalil was almost certainly an Arab, or at least of Arabian descent. Thailand might be his home base, but she could only guess how far this sex slave trafficking web she'd fallen into reached.

These thoughts flitted through Leah's rational mind at lightning speed, but were quickly edged out by raw emotion, the top one being fear.

Alex nodded calmly and knelt gracefully beside the tub, his movements somehow feminine. Lifting a tube from the side of the tub, he squeezed a dollop of what looked like shampoo into his hand. "I will wash your hair," he informed her. His voice, too, was feminine, both in tone and quality. His large brown eyes reminded

Leah of a deer and his beard, if he even shaved at all, was very light.

Leah would much rather have washed her own hair but she didn't protest, the memory of the beatings at the hands of the men now standing guard far too fresh in her mind. Instead, she dunked her head back into the fragrant water, closing her eyes with pleasure as it sluiced over her.

When she lifted her head, Alex leaned over her and rubbed the shampoo into her scalp. The shorter guard brought over a large pitcher and stood waiting. Alex massaged her scalp gently as he shampooed the tangled mess of her hair.

Looking up, he nodded toward the guard holding the pitcher, who poured fresh warm water over Leah's head. They repeated the process. Alex then selected a washcloth from a pile that rested on the wide rim of the huge tub. Using a bar of sweetly scented soap, he washed every inch of Leah's body. Unlike the stoic, masklike faces of the guards, Alex smiled in a rather absent way as he cleaned her body. Leah had the odd feeling of being bathed by a kindly but disinterested grandmother.

She regarded the man surreptitiously as he worked, noting his chubby, beardless face, pudgy fingers and feminine gestures, and suddenly realized what she was seeing. This man was a eunuch!

Leah, familiar with Muslim and Turkish history, recalled that eunuchs were employed in a sultan's harem to keep the ladies in line, while harboring no sexual desires of their own, or at least no ability to act on them. She had no idea such a barbaric practice as castration still existed, but then, she'd had no idea harems still existed either.

The experience of being bathed by this castrated man while the guards stood by was strange in the extreme. When Alex was done, he nodded toward the taller guard.

"Get out," the guard ordered Leah. Turning to Alex, he added, "Do a good job. If the steward finds her worthy, she will be presented once again to the Master." Leah imagined she could actually hear the capital M in the way he said the word.

What if she was found unworthy? Would they kill her outright? More likely they'd put her to work as a prostitute, in conditions far worse than this luxurious marbled bathroom hinted at.

Having little choice, Leah stepped out of the tub and stood passively as Alex toweled her dry. The guards then led her to a sink, directing her to stand beside it with her legs shoulder-width apart, her arms extended over her head. Soft cuffs that closed with Velcro were secured around her wrists and clipped to chains hanging from a fixture in the ceiling.

For a moment Leah was afraid she was in for another beating. But instead of producing a whip, one of the men filled the sink with hot water and dropped a washcloth into it while Alex rubbed a thick, creamy paste under Leah's arms. She tried to stay very still as he used a razor to scrape away any stubble.

When he was done, he knelt in front of Leah and began to snip away her pubic curls with a small pair of scissors. He rubbed her mons with a damp cloth and then smoothed more of the shaving cream over her sex. Leah closed her eyes, her face burning with humiliation as the man shaved her pussy while the implacable guards stared down at them. Alex was gentle and careful, still appearing completely disinterested in what he was doing, as if he were peeling a piece of fruit or washing one of the household pets. The objectification was at once unsettling and a relief.

Apparently satisfied, Alex eventually moved on to her legs, shaving them smooth. His touch was careful and expert, as if he'd done this many times before. When he was finished, the guards led her to a padded stool in front of a mirrored counter and had her sit, Alex following behind.

On the counter were several large trays filled with all kinds of makeup, including numerous bottles of foundation, blush, lipsticks, eyeliners and mascara, as well as a dozen hairbrushes and combs. Alex selected a round brush and produced a blow dryer from beneath the counter, with which he proceeded to dry Leah's long, thick hair.

As he worked, Leah stared into her own large, frightened eyes in the mirror. There were blue smudges of fatigue beneath her eyes and her skin was mottled with sunburn from having spent the morning out in the kennel. Her lips were reddened and chapped and her mouth was pinched with fear.

She looked away.

When Alex was done with her hair, he pulled it back into a hairclip and pivoted the stool so she was facing him. He began to apply makeup, something Leah almost never wore. He started with foundation, using a small makeup sponge and moving it in circular sweeps over her throat, cheeks and forehead. He added blush, eyeliner, eye shadow, mascara and lipstick, taking a long time on her eyes. Leah imagined herself being turned into some kind of absurdly over-painted whore.

But when he spun her back around to release the clip from her hair, Leah was startled at the transformation—the blue smudges were erased, the sunburned smoothed to a dewy glow, her lips a soft, inviting pink. The blue of her eyes was set off by kohl blue eyeliner and sparkling silver eye shadow.

Finally, using a small brush dipped into a pot of rouge, Alex painted Leah's pink nipples to a dark rose color. Next, she was led to a large wardrobe set against the far wall of the bathroom. A white silk robe, so sheer it was see-through, was draped over her shoulders.

"The steward will inspect you for flaws. If you please him, he may invite you to dine with him. If you displease him..." The guard trailed off, and Leah almost thought she saw him shudder.

This involuntary action, more than anything he could have said, caused an icy rivulet of terror to trickle along Leah's spine. She had a horrible feeling her punishment would go far beyond just being denied the chance to share a meal with this steward person. She knew she'd damn well better please him, whatever it took.

In fact, she was certain her very life depended on it.

Chapter 6

"I tell you, Reg, I'm worried sick. I think something's happened to her."

After another fruitless visit to the local police, Devin called his longtime friend, Reggie Smith, who had lived in Thailand for the last decade and owned a string of convenience stores that specialized in British and European goods. They agreed to meet at a local pub that was a favorite among the British expats in Pattaya. Reggie had ordered lunch for them both but Devin had no appetite.

As Devin began to relate the story of the missing Leah and his suspicions that there was foul play afoot, Reggie joked, "I know you're god's gift to women, Dev, but could it be the lady found a better offer? Did that even enter your egotistic mind?" He quickly sobered as Devin filled him in on the details, including the fact Leah had now been missing for at least twenty-four hours.

"Wait a minute. Which hotel did you say it was?" Reggie asked, narrowing his eyes.

"The Pattaya Gold. I've been staying there while I closed a beachfront deal."

"The Pattaya Gold, huh?" Reggie squinted at the ceiling, pursing his lips. "That name rings a definite bell.

Let me just check something." He pulled out his smart phone and busied himself for a few moments while Devin stared at the untouched food on his plate.

Reggie looked up from his phone. "I thought so. That's the one that was in the news last year. An American woman by the name of Jane Erwin disappeared from that very hotel. Caused a big stink in the international community. She'd checked in alone — her husband was to join her later in the month, once he'd finished up some business or other — but she apparently checked out four days after she'd arrived, according to the staff. Disappeared without a trace. The local police, notoriously corrupt, couldn't find a single lead. The husband, at his wits end, hired a local private investigator who I happen to know, but I don't think the guy made much headway either. Odds are pretty good she was sold off to one of the sex rings that run rampant in this country. Either that or she's dead."

"Oh my god. Do you think that's what happened to Leah?" Devin heard the panic in his voice.

Reggie leaned forward, his expression serious. "These sex traffic rings are insidious. They mostly focus on local girls — girls who won't be much missed, or whose families need the money so badly they just hand them over like chattel. But every once in a while you see a story in the paper about a European or American disappearing. Probably for every one that makes the news, there are two dozen others never reported.

"I've got to do something. I've got to find her! The police—"

"I wouldn't waste any more time there," Reggie interrupted. "I have a better idea. You should contact that PI I know—see whatever happened with that case. Maybe he could provide some direction."

"What's his name?"

"George Sirir-something or other I could never pronounce. Wait a second." Shifting, Reggie reached into his jacket and extracted a long, narrow wallet. Opening it, he rummaged for a few moments. "Aha. Here it is. I have his card. He did some surveillance work for me in a couple of my stores where some employee theft was going on."

Devin took the business card and read it: *George Siriratsivawong: Investigations. Discretion Assured.* "I won't even try to pronounce that," Devin said.

"We just call him George S."

"I recognize that as a Thai surname, but George?"

Reggie shrugged. "His mother's British, father is Thai. I'm afraid he's more Thai than British when it comes to having his palm crossed with silver for information. I know he got pretty heavily involved in the investigation for a while there. No doubt the money, and hence his interest, dried up before anything came of it. Still, it's a place to start. Just make sure you bring plenty of cash."

Devin looked at the card again. "There's a phone number but no address."

Reggie nodded. "Yeah, he does a lot of bar girl checks. Discretion is the name of his game. He vets anyone before letting them get too close."

"Forgive my ignorance, but what are bar girl checks?"

"A lot of guys who fly in regularly from abroad meet girls in the go-go bars. Most of these dancers are hookers on the side, which is where the real money is. Some of these blokes like to have one special girl when they come to town. They will pay for the girl's rent and other stuff in exchange for a promise that she doesn't step out with other guys for money while he's away. But you know," Reggie gave a broad wink, "once the cat's away, the mice will play, especially when there are mouths to feed. These losers get suspicious and hire George to check out their bar girl's story. They want to make sure they're keeping their legs closed."

"That sounds pretty sleazy to me," Devin said.

Reggie shrugged. "Hey, this is Pattaya, not London. You want to find Leah, you're gonna have to get down into the trenches with people who have connections and know the local scene."

Devin already had his mobile out, more than ready to get down into the trenches if it meant finding Leah.

~*~

The room was elegant but austere, with a dark, shiny hardwood floor and pale gray walls with white trim molding. The space was windowless, lit by tall brass floor lamps. The only furniture in the room was a single chair made of black, shiny teakwood, and a circular raised dais covered with a black mat set directly in front of it.

Sitting in the chair was a tall, angular man with a shaved head and a black goatee and mustache. He wore a single, large diamond stud in one earlobe. His fingers, long and slender, were tented just below his chin, lending him a contemplative air. He was staring at Leah as she was brought into the room, his eyes dark and glittering, his expression inscrutable.

The guards lifted her onto the dais and stepped back a respectful distance. Leah stood on what she would have described as an auction block in front of the steward, feeling both frightened and ridiculous.

"Drop the robe and lift your hands behind your head." He spoke in the same cultured, British accent as the man they referred to as Master, though there was more of a hint of what Leah guessed was his native Arabic in the guttural turn of his vowels and the way he rolled his r's.

While Leah's rational brain, which was highly sensitive to linguistic nuance, was busy identifying the man's accent, it took a moment longer to process what he had just ordered her to do. Aware she had no choice in the matter, Leah let the silky robe fall from her shoulders. Lifting her arms, she clasped her fingers together behind her neck.

The man's eyes moved slowly over her bare body, resting a while on her breasts before moving in a sweep over every inch. Leah felt thoroughly violated by his relentless gaze. "Turn to the right," he ordered, and then, "Now to the left."

Leah's stomach burbled audibly and she felt suddenly light headed from hunger. *If you please him, he may invite you to dine with him.* Leah refused to contemplate the second half of the guard's promise, or, rather, his threat, instead focusing her mind on the hope of food. If she pleased this man, this steward, she would get to eat. That was what mattered now — she had to get some food in her body to keep up her strength while she figured a way out.

"Turn completely around," the steward ordered. He spoke in a quiet, almost lazy way, for some reason recalling to her mind *The Jungle Book* animated movie she'd loved as a child, when the evil snake Kaa had hissed, "trussssst in meeee," to the unsuspecting Mowgli.

Leah turned, bringing the ever-present guards into her line of sight. The guards were standing with arms folded, like statues on either side of the door, their eyes straight ahead.

"Bend over and grab your ankles," the steward ordered. Leah felt her cheeks flaming, but she did as she was told, reminding herself this was a means to an end, a way to stay alive.

In spite of her resolve to get through this, her legs and arms had begun to shake, fear, hunger and exhaustion taking their toll. She wasn't sure how much longer she could maintain this embarrassing position and was greatly relieved when the steward said, "Stand and turn again to face me, arms at your sides."

With relief, Leah straightened and turned slowly until she was again facing the steward. He sat back and tilted his head as he continued to scrutinize her. Leah wasn't sure she could hang on much longer, being stared at as if she was an animal or a piece of furniture he was considering buying.

Finally he spoke. "Though imperfect, you are passable. With some work and training, you might be acceptable to the Master." He stood, adding, "Put on your robe. I am going to break my fast. Would you care to join me?"

Leah had a sudden, vivid fantasy of whipping out a Samurai sword, like Uma Thurman in the movie, *Kill Bill*. She would leap from the dais, sword swinging, and lop off this arrogant man's head. Then, whipping around, she would skewer both guards, running them through with the sword and pinning them, like shish kebob, to the wall.

Focus on what you can control. Food. He is offering food.

Bending down, she reached for the silk robe, pulling it over her shoulders and wrapping it around her body.

"Yes, please," she managed in what she hoped was a submissive tone. She cleared her throat, forcing herself to add, "Thank you, sir."

The steward nodded slightly in the direction of the guards. Leah was lifted from the dais. The guards flanked her on either side as they followed the steward through a door that led into a second room.

Leah's senses were at once assailed with the smell of roasting coffee. Sunlight was sparkling through a large window that faced the water. A circular table covered in white linen, like the one in the Master's bedroom, was set for what looked like afternoon tea, or, in this case, coffee. There was a plate with peeled oranges and another piled with finger sandwiches filled with various pastes and vegetables. Beside them was a tray of what Leah recognized as baklava, a delicious pastry of filo dough, honey, cinnamon and walnuts. Next to the food sat two small china cups and a brass samovar Leah assumed held coffee.

There were two chairs, one on either side of the table. The steward sat down. Nearly faint with hunger, Leah started to sink into the other chair, but a firm hand pushed hard on her shoulder, forcing her to her knees.

The steward regarded her, lifting an eyebrow. "Untrained, impertinent American. Slaves never sit on furniture uninvited. You may kneel on the cushion."

Fuck you, you arrogant prick!

Leah tried to keep her face impassive, aware by the man's sudden frown that her anger had probably been obvious. She couldn't fuck up now, not when she was so close to being given food. She scooted toward the flat silk cushion she now noticed on the floor beside the steward's chair, taking small comfort that at least she wasn't being required to kneel on the hard wood.

There was another nearly imperceptible nod from the steward toward the guards, who withdrew from the room, closing the door softly behind them. The steward lifted the samovar and poured dark, rich coffee into the tiny cups. He stirred in sugar from a silver pot and held one of the cups out to Leah.

She took it, sipping the strong, sweet coffee, her eyes on the food. She watched hungrily as the steward selected a sandwich with what looked like cheese and cucumber on two thin slices of bread from the plate. Leah's mouth began to water uncontrollably as she watched him lift the sandwich to his mouth and pop it in.

He selected a second sandwich. This one he ate more slowly, his gaze on the window as he chewed. When he had eaten four of the tiny sandwiches, he took the orange and split it in half, eating several segments one at a time.

Leah was ready to scream. She wanted to spring on the man like a wild animal and topple him from the chair. Then she would grab handfuls of the food and eat and eat until she was finally full. He was taunting her by making her sit at his feet like a dog, waiting patiently for scraps.

And yet, that was just what she was doing, and she knew she'd better keep doing it if she hoped to get those scraps. This was a test, she was sure of it. And she would pass it if at all possible.

Finally, almost as an afterthought as he sipped his second cup of coffee, the steward turned his gaze to her. "Would you care for a sandwich? Perhaps a bit of fruit?"

"Yes, please," she whispered fervently.

The steward held out his hand and Leah realized he wanted her empty cup back. She complied, watching with hungry eyes as he set three of the small sandwiches and half an orange on a plate.

When he handed it to her, Leah took it with shaking hands. She ate the orange first. The fruit was juicy and sweet, and very quickly gone. She tried to savor the different cheeses and raw vegetables and fresh bread of the dainty little sandwiches, but she was too hungry to do much more than wolf them down.

She realized the steward was watching her with an amused expression. "Would you care for a piece of baklava?"

"Yes, please."

The steward selected a plump piece that was oozing with honey and set it down on her now empty plate. She bit into the delicious confection, the sweetness exploding in her mouth. With food finally in her stomach, she was able to savor the dessert, one of her favorites.

The steward poured another cup of the strong coffee and stirred in some sugar. He handed her the cup. Leah sipped it. She would have loved another ten or twelve of those finger sandwiches and at least three more pieces of the pastry but nothing more was offered. Instead, the steward patted his lips with a linen napkin and rose from his seat.

A quick, sharp clap of his hands brought the guards back into the room. "Take the girl to the assessment chamber. I am interested in testing her tolerance of sexual pain for the Master."

Leah was hustled along yet another hallway of the huge house, the food she'd eaten now sitting like lead in her belly. She was brought into a large room filled with all kinds of equipment, including whipping posts, wooden stocks, a spanking horse, a bondage table and other wicked looking apparatus that, even with her experience with BDSM, Leah didn't have a name for.

She gasped when she saw the long, low sleep cage. Inside was a young woman lying on her side. She was naked, with silver cuffs on her wrists and ankles like the ones Alex had worn, a silver slave collar around her neck. She had long, straight black hair, narrow, dark eyes and a wide, sensuous mouth. She was clutching the bars of the cage, watching silently as Leah was led into the room.

The steward entered the room a moment later. Ignoring the caged girl, he said in his soft, serpentine voice, "Remove her robe and secure the girl to the suspension rack. Then bring me the quirt."

Leah was propelled to the center of room. Her robe was pulled from her and she was forced to stand on a small platform beneath chains that hung from the ceiling, leather cuffs at their ends. She was cuffed in place, her arms pulled taut overhead. Her ankles were cuffed to eyebolts on the platform, her legs spread far apart.

Leah's breath was coming fast, her heart racing in fearful anticipation. Though she was no stranger to erotic BDSM play, it had always been consensual and on her terms. Hadn't she already been "assessed" at the hands of the guards? She had a feeling the steward had something different in mind and she didn't like the sound of it one little bit.

She watched with trepidation as one of the guards went to a wall hung with an assortment of whips. He returned to the steward and held out a whip with a braided leather handle and two long, thin strips of leather Leah knew from experience could sting like hell on contact.

The guard handed the quirt to the steward, who nodded brusquely. "You may wait outside. I'll let you know when you are needed." The two men withdrew, closing the door behind them. Leah was alone with the steward and the naked, caged girl, who had remained utterly silent, her wide eyes fixed on Leah.

The steward moved to stand directly in front of Leah, the quirt in his hand. "The Master has certain tastes. He values girls who can take a good beating without crying out. He especially values girls who can derive sexual pleasure from erotic pain." He drew the leather tips of the quirt over Leah's bare breasts and leaned in close.

"American girls are willful and noncompliant. It is rare that they prove themselves worthy of the Master's attentions. More often than not, they are sold to the highest bidder for the exotic gentlemen's clubs or, if they aren't even worthy of that, they will be consigned to the brothels that litter this country."

Leah shuddered as the steward drew the quirt down her body. "He has plenty of Asian girls like Setsuko." He waved toward the girl in the cage. "These women understand the value and duty of proper submission. Though," he smiled dryly, "they do sometimes need reminding and punishment."

He turned toward Setsuko. "Roll over and show the American girl your stripes."

The girl released the bars and rolled obediently onto her other side. Leah drew in her breath as she took in the welts on the girl's back and ass. There were easily a dozen long, red, ridged lines, probably caused by a cane. Several of the welts had cut the flesh, and the girl's skin was smeared with dried blood. Leah wondered what she had done, or failed to do, to earn such a harsh punishment.

Setsuko apparently forgotten, the steward turned his focus back to Leah. "A golden-haired beauty would be a nice addition to the Master's harem. Especially one who can tolerate pain."

Though she didn't relish the idea of entering the Master's harem, it seemed a better alternative to being sold to the highest bidder to serve out her days in an exotic club or whorehouse. At least given what she knew of harems from what she'd read, the women were confined in luxurious quarters and afforded relative freedom within those confines. It had to be better and certainly safer than being whored out on the street.

Stepping back, the steward struck Leah's left breast with the quirt, leaving two stinging lines of fire in its wake. Leah jerked and gasped, breathing hard through her nose to keep from yelping as she gripped the chains above the wrist cuffs.

The man nodded in apparent approval, while lifting his eyebrows as if surprised. He struck her again, this time across the front of both her thighs. Leah winced and bit her lower lip to keep from crying out. The steward pursed his lips as he regarded her, as if thinking what to do next.

He walked out of her line of vision. She could see the girl in the cage, who was again facing her, her fingers wrapped around the bars. The girl silently mouthed something Leah couldn't catch. Distracted by this, Leah wasn't ready for the next stroke, a hard lash across her ass, and she cried out.

She was ready, though, when the next stroke came, landing just above first. This time, however, the tips of the quirt curled painfully around her left hip, drawing tears to her eyes. The steward struck her several times across her back and Leah felt herself edging toward panic, pain and fear rising like a bubble from inside her, threatening to burst out in a howl.

Breathe. Let go. I can feel your tension. Hold nothing back.

Leah startled, glancing sharply around the room. The voice was that of Jean Luc, her only lover since Todd. Though the relationship had only lasted a few weeks, ending with his return to his native country of France, during that time Jean Luc had taught her in a hands-on way about using erotic pain to reach that heavenly place where pleasure and suffering fused into a sublime experience.

The steward was focusing on the backs of her thighs now, a thousand bee stings moving in relentless waves over her skin. Cuffed to the platform as she was, she couldn't even try to twist away from the onslaught.

Again she heard the voice, which of course was entirely in her head. *Flow with the pain. Let it take you where you need to go. Show me your grace. Show me your courage.*

Leah felt her eyelids fluttering closed. The sting of the quirt, while still painful, was somehow more tolerable. She took a deep breath and expelled it slowly.

That's it. Do it for me. Do it for us.

Her head felt suddenly heavy, too heavy to hold upright. She let it fall back and felt her lips parting as a soft sigh escaped them.

Yes. You're nearly there. Take the last leap and let yourself fly...

The steward had moved in front of her again, his quirt striking like snake bites against her breasts. It hurt, oh yes, it hurt, but at the same time she felt a deep, sensual peace settle over her like a gossamer net, enfolding her and keeping her safe.

She saw the endless blue sparkling ocean beneath her as she soared away from the pain. The leather tips still struck relentlessly over her breasts, stomach and thighs, but Leah no longer felt the sting.

She was flying.

She was free.

Chapter 7

After Devin established himself as a friend of Reggie Smith, George had been forthcoming about his location, which turned out to be only fifteen minutes by cab from the pub. After a quick stop at the local bank where his company did business, Devin directed the cabbie to the address George had given him.

The private investigator's office was a small, crowded space located on a narrow street, wedged between a dry goods store and a hair salon. George S. was a small, trim man of about fifty. He wore a white straw fedora and had a cigarette hanging out of the corner of his mouth. The once-white walls of the cluttered office were yellowed with years of nicotine and the air was stale.

Reminding himself that beggars couldn't be choosers, Devin sat down on one of the folding chairs set in front of the metal desk, which was piled high with folders and scattered papers.

After the obligatory greetings and discussion of their shared acquaintance of Reggie Smith, Devin dived in, explaining his concerns while George scribbled on a yellow legal pad, the cigarette still dangling. When Devin mentioned the cold case of the other missing American woman, the PI perked up.

"Ah, yes. I'm quite familiar with that particular hotel. I have collected much useful information. Jane Erwin wasn't the first to go missing. There here have been at least five other girls in the past four years who've vanished into thin air after either working at or staying in that hotel."

Devin leaned forward, hanging on George's words, desperate to hear more. But George only took another drag on his cigarette and smiled politely in Devin's direction.

Devin realized he was waiting to be paid for his information, as Reg had predicted. "Oh, right," Devin faltered, and then, catching himself, made sure to phrase his offer in the proper polite terms that wouldn't offend, while still making his intentions clear.

"Mr. Smith has spoken quite highly of your skill and ability to collect useful information. I would be most honored to offer recompense for your hard-won knowledge."

George shook a cigarette from a crumpled packet of Marlboros, using the butt of his last one to light a fresh cigarette. He blew out a smoke ring while Devin struggled to keep his patience. "You are too kind, Mr. Lyons," the man finally said. "I am honored you would consider me worthy."

Devin had no idea if the man was in fact worthy, but clearly he wasn't going to find out unless he shelled out some cash. He reached for the envelope he'd filled at the bank and opened it, extracting a thick wad of Thai baht that approximated one hundred British pounds, aware the PI would probably bargain up the amount before the deal was done.

He set the money on the desk between them. "I would greatly appreciate access to your files on the investigations you have made on behalf of Jane Erwin and the other missing women. That's five thousand baht for your troubles."

George looked down at the money without reaching for it. He looked up slowly, the polite smile still pasted on his face. "You are most generous, I am sure." He kept his hands folded on the desk, still making no move to reach for the money. "I have an entire file drawer devoted to the topic. Hundreds of hours have been spent on this investigation. What you're asking for is very valuable information, Mr. Lyons."

Information you were paid to track down, Devin thought, but said nothing. He opened the envelope again and pulled out the rest of the money. "Forgive me, I didn't appreciate just how valuable that information must be." Making it clear the envelope was now empty, he said, "Another five thousand for your trouble."

George's polite smile broadened into a bona fide grin as he reached for the pile of money while Devin hid his sigh of relief that it was enough. For all he knew, he was buying a bunch of useless paper and dead-end leads.

He watched eagerly as George leaned over and pulled open the bottom drawer of the battered metal filing cabinet. George extracted three manila folders stuffed with papers and set them on the desk between them.

Devin started to reach for the files, but George had placed his hands on them as he leaned forward. Devin struggled to maintain his patience, aware he'd get more information if he let the man go at his own pace. "I've never been able to prove any of it," George said earnestly, "but I've learned a lot in the process, let me tell you. I got really close with the Jane Erwin case, but I got shut down by officials who didn't want me to succeed for reasons of their own."

"You got close? How so?"

"I've found a trail of evidence leading to what I believe is an international trafficking ring that specializes in foreign women, especially English, French and American, but works the local population as well. It's rumored they provide a steady supply of girls to an Arab millionaire who lives somewhere on the Thai coast. I managed to talk to a Thai girl who was brought briefly to the compound, but she was rejected for whatever reason. Last I heard she was working in a local strip club."

"You've talked to a woman who was taken to the compound? Why didn't she go to the police? Why is this allowed to go on?" Even as he asked this, Devin knew how naïve he sounded. As long as there had been so-called civilization, there had been slavery, sexual and otherwise, and not just in the Far East. A little thing like the law didn't deter criminals intent on trafficking in human life.

George was shaking his head and rubbing his finger and thumb together. "Money, my friend. It all comes down to money. Too many palms are getting too much grease to stop what is a very lucrative operation for a lot of people."

Still focused on the man's earlier comments, Devin pressed, "Where is this compound? Have you been there?"

George shook his head. "Never found the place, though I have some hunches. It's all there in my notes." Finally he lifted his hands from the files and pushed them slowly across the cluttered desk toward Devin.

"Good luck. You'll need it."

~*~

Leah came slowly, unwillingly, back to earth. She had literally left the premises, at least her spirit had, during that brief but lovely interlude when she'd been completely submerged within her own submissive headspace.

Now she became aware of the stiff leather cuffs that were cutting uncomfortably into her wrists. Her head was still back, eyes still closed, but she felt the presence of someone standing just in front of her.

"Impressive," the steward hissed softly, recalling her completely back to the present. "Forgive me, Leah. I had underestimated you."

Leah.

The use of her name caused Leah to snap her head upright, and her eyes flew open. The steward was regarding her with a grave smile. "You have proved yourself more worthy than I dared dream. You accepted the whipping with a grace I have rarely seen. I had no idea you were adept at the submissive arts."

As the endorphins from the experience began to ebb away, Leah was becoming aware of the fiery lines of stinging pain that crisscrossed her flesh from shoulder to thigh, both front and back. Her mouth was dry and she longed for a drink of water. Sweat was trickling down her sides and if she hadn't been held up by her wrists, she would have collapsed. She wanted nothing more than to be let down from the chains. She longed to curl into a ball somewhere safe and far, far away from this nightmare place.

The steward clapped his hands and the ubiquitous guards appeared. "Let her down and take her to the bath, and then put her in a waiting cell. She will be presented to the Master this evening. Make sure she is properly prepared."

The two men released her cuffs and half-led, half-carried the stumbling girl from the room. She was led back to the huge, opulent bathroom and permitted to use the toilet again while the bath was drawn.

Gratefully she sank down into the fragrant, soft warmth of the welcoming water, not even minding the sting as it made contact with her tender, welted skin.

Again Alex was summoned, and again she was bathed, her hair washed as before. When she was placed before the mirror, Alex used a soft cloth and an emollient cream to wipe away the remaining makeup. He left her hair wet, pulling it back from her face with a dark blue ribbon. She was given a matching blue robe and led from the room.

She realized she was being taken to the waiting cell the steward had referenced. She fully expected to be thrust into a cage, with perhaps a canvas cot or a pallet of straw for a bed. No matter how mean the accommodations, at least she hoped she would be left in peace for a little while before being *presented* to the Master.

She was led down the hallway to another set of stairs, much narrower than those leading from the first to the second floor. Instead of a prison, the room she was led to, though small, was actually quite comfortable. There wasn't space for much more than a single bed, but it had clean, white sheets and two plump pillows. The walls were painted a soothing, pale blue and there was a thickly piled royal blue throw rug on the floor beside the bed. The room had no windows, but a lamp beside the bed cast a peaceful glow.

The guards left her alone there, shutting and locking the door behind them. Leah stood in the center of the tiny room, wondering if there was anything here she could use as a weapon. The mattress was placed in an iron bed frame. She could tear the sheet into strips and use them to strangle the guards when they came in. Or she could use the brass lamp to smash their heads in.

These ideas, of course, were fantasy. There was no way she could overpower the two thugs, even if she hadn't been kept terrorized, caged, beaten and nearly starved for the past twenty-four hours or however long it had been.

She lay down on the mattress, which was surprisingly comfortable. The sheets were of the softest cotton, the pillows filled with down. How long had she been held captive? She tried to think. She had been abducted in the afternoon, and had spent a hideous night beneath the stairs. In the morning, she'd been taken to the Master, and then hauled off to the kennels. Based on the food she'd been served by the steward, and the slant of the sun through the window, it had been late afternoon. The whipping session, while it had seemed to go on for hours, had probably been more like thirty minutes. Then the second bath, and now she was here.

The Master would probably call for her after his dinner. Heavens only knew when she would next be offered a meal. At least for now she was clean and, while not exactly full, no longer starving. What she could see of the welts the steward had left with his quirt were already fading. Most importantly, though, she was still alive.

Leah felt her eyes closing as she sank into the soft, inviting comfort of the bed. She knew she needed to be thinking, planning, somehow figuring a way out of this mess. She needed to keep her wits about her if she was going to make good her escape.

But she was tired, so tired. She recalled a line from a book she'd once read: *Sleep is a weapon*. Right now, it was the only weapon she had. Closing her eyes, she slept.

Leah awoke to the sound of a key scraping in the door lock. She reached for her cell phone to check the time, wondering who was bothering her in the middle of the night. Hadn't she left a *do not disturb* sign on her doorknob?

She came fully awake as the door opened, reality slamming into her like a two-by-four. She stopped reaching for the phantom night table and the nonexistent cell phone and sat up, her breath coming in shallow gasps.

She expected the twin thugs to appear, but instead it was the steward, with Alex just behind him. Alex was carrying what looked like a large makeup bag. The steward was carrying a large porcelain bowl in his hands and a red velvet bag slung over one arm.

The steward set the bowl on the floor at the end of the bed. "Up, up," he said briskly, sharply clapping his hands. "The Master is ready for you." Leah stood on rubbery legs. The steward pointed toward the bowl.

"Empty your bladder. Then kneel on the rug so Alex can attend to your makeup and hair."

Leah did have to pee, but the thought of squatting over a bowl in front of these men was not a pleasant one. Aware she had no choice, however, she moved to the end of the bed and positioned herself awkwardly over the makeshift toilet. It was several seconds before her muscles relaxed enough to allow her to pee in front of the men, both of whom were watching her. She felt her face heating as the stream of urine finally splashed into the bowl and she turned her head to the wall, closing her eyes.

When she was done, Alex handed her some tissue, which she used to wipe herself. "Do you need to move your bowels?" the steward asked. Leah shook her head, glad she did not.

The steward moved quickly, striking her left cheek with a hard slap. Gasping in pain and surprise, Leah nearly toppled the porcelain bowl as she jumped back. "You will answer a direct question!" the steward barked. "The Master will not tolerate this kind of insubordination. You'd better learn now, or the price will be much steeper than a mere tap to your cheek, I assure you."

"Yes, sir!" Leah cried, her heart thumping.

Alex, his face placid and bland, as if nothing unusual was happening, was setting out makeup and brushes on a black lacquer tray he placed beside the throw rug in front of Leah's bed.

The steward pointed to the rug. "Kneel at attention, hands clasped behind your back." Leah scrambled to obey, her cheek stinging. Kneeling in front of Leah, first Alex brushed her hair and used barrettes that sparkled with what looked like diamonds and sapphires to pin it back on either side of Leah's face. Alex applied makeup as he had earlier, including brushing her nipples with rouge. All the while the steward stood by, watching the two of them with hooded eyes.

When Alex was done, he packed the makeup and tray back into his large bag and rose gracefully. Retrieving the porcelain bowl, he bowed to the steward and glided silently from the room.

"Stand up," the steward ordered, sliding the velvet bag from his arm. From it he took two sets of silver cuffs and a silver slave collar, identical to the ones Alex and the girl in the cage wore. The cuffs were really more like narrow bracelets, though with an added O ring. He placed the cuffs on Leah's wrists and ankles, clicking them into place.

"Lift your hair," he commanded.

When he placed the collar around her throat, the hasp snicked closed with the finality of a gun being cocked, causing a shudder to move involuntarily through Leah's body.

Instinctively she reached for the collar, tugging at it as the panic rose in her gut. "No!" she cried softly before she could stop herself. She couldn't let this happen.

"Hands at your sides," the steward snapped, using the O ring on her wrist cuff to jerk her hand away. "I would beat you for that outburst but the Master is waiting. You are being honored, foolish girl. The Master only accepts a select few each year into his harem. Most of the girls we are brought are not found worthy. Be glad of your blond hair and flawless skin. Revel in your ability to tolerate pain with grace. I've been easy on you, but the Master has very high standards. If you disappoint him by misbehaving in any way, you will have *me* to answer to."

The cold threat in his voice chilled Leah to the bone.

"We will practice your entrance," he continued. "When you enter the room, you are to approach the Master and kneel in slave greeting at his feet. I will instruct you." He pointed to the ground. "Lower yourself as gracefully as you can. Think of a ballet dancer. Move slowly, always presenting your body with shoulders back and chin lifted."

Leah tried to obey, his threat still ringing loud in her ears. "No, no! You move like a field laborer. Where is your grace! Get up and try it again." Leah forced herself up on shaking legs. Finally on the fourth try, the steward was satisfied.

"That is the first part of the slave greeting. Next," he instructed, "you lean forward slowly, bringing your forehead to the floor, your arms stretched in front of you, fingers spread flat against the ground. You must use this slave greeting every time you come into the

Master's presence and don't move until he gives you permission."

Leah tried to obey, feeling ridiculous. This asshole Khalil clearly had some gargantuan delusions of grandeur, which the steward and everyone else he kept around him appeared more than happy to perpetuate.

The steward made her practice the so-called slave greeting over and over until she wanted to scream. Finally he glanced at the gold watch on his wrist. "You are not yet adept, but it will have to do. The Master must not be kept waiting."

A hand on her shoulder, the steward led her from the room. She was again brought into Khalil's bedroom. He was sitting in a large chair, his expression as imperious as an emperor's as he watched them enter.

"Remember your grace. Now go!" the steward hissed into her ear. He gave her shoulder a small push.

Leah approached Khalil unsteadily, keenly aware of her nudity and her rouged nipples, praying she could pull off this kneeling nonsense without collapsing. The steward's threat was still ringing in her ears. *You will have* me *to answer to.* She heard the door closing quietly behind her, but didn't dare turn around to see if the steward had remained in the room.

Khalil was wearing a yellow silk robe and, as far as she could tell, nothing else. His lips were lifted in a small, smug smile. Leah imagined hurling herself at him and knocking him from his chair. She wanted to pummel his handsome face, gouge out his eyes, kick him hard in the nuts and see how much grace *he* managed while she beat him to a pulp.

When she got to the little rug in front of Khalil, she lowered herself the way the steward had showed her. Leaning forward, she touched the floor with her forehead and stretched out her arms, splaying her fingers as she'd been instructed. She stayed in that position for several long seconds, her heart beating rapidly, hating the arrogant man she imagined was staring down at her.

"You may rise, little one," Khalil said in his deep, well-modulated voice, as if he were some kind of fucking king.

Leah lifted herself from the floor and stood, trying to keep the rage and fear from her face. She wouldn't give the bastard the satisfaction. The man was staring at her with a hungry look, his eyes hooded. "I confess my weakness for such golden beauty, a rarity in my country. I have waited a long time for a girl such as you."

Khalil stood, undoing the sash of his robe and letting it fall from his shoulders. He was naked beneath it, his long, thick cock fully erect. Leah took a step back, wrapping her arms around her torso. Khalil frowned, his thick brows coming together over his beautiful eyes. "*Never* cover yourself in front of me, little one." He spoke softly, but there was steel in his tone. Frightened, Leah dropped her arms.

He sat again, his cock bobbing proudly between his muscular thighs. "You will make a wonderful addition to my harem. My steward spoke highly of your ability to suffer with grace and I look forward to exploring this fully." He rubbed his hands together and licked his lips, as if contemplating a feast while Leah was left to absorb what he'd said.

Dropping his hands to his thighs, he continued, "But that will wait. For now, come kneel in front of me and worship my cock. If you please me, you will be rewarded. If you do not," he paused, his dark eyes flashing, "you will be properly punished."

Leah pressed her lips together, aware she had no choice. Maybe she could bite the bastard's cock off and shove it in his mouth before making her getaway. She knew even if she managed such a bloody feat, she would be stopped and probably killed instantly. For a moment she almost felt it would be worth it.

But her desire to live was stronger than her anger or her fear, and so she knelt in front of her captor and leaned tentatively forward. "It is well known you American girls love to suck cock," Khalil stated. "Take it deep. Use your hands as you wish. *Please* me, little one."

The *or else* he'd left unspoken hung menacingly in the air between them. Leah reached for the naked man's balls, cupping them lightly in trembling fingers, forcing down the nearly overwhelming impulse to crush them.

A drop of pre-come balanced on the fat head of his imposing cock. Closing her eyes and holding her breath, Leah opened her mouth and slid her lips over the head and partway down the thick, hard shaft.

In point of fact, despite his obnoxious, sweeping and incorrect statement that all American women love to suck cock, Leah in fact did enjoy the practice, and prided herself on her skill in that regard. She loved the swell of a rising shaft against her tongue, and the way she could reduce a man to trembling, moaning jelly in her hands.

But that was with men *she* chose, on her own terms, not when being held against her will and basically having her mouth raped. *Get through it. You can do this. Focus on the slave girl fantasy. Pretend this is a dream.*

The slave girl fantasy. What incredible irony! Leah, sexually masochistic and submissive by nature, had developed an elaborate fantasy in her teens when masturbating, in which she was the pampered and beloved slave of a fabulously handsome Dom. He would mark her daily with a whip or cane, keep her naked and in chains, and fuck and sexually torture her nonstop, all the while murmuring delicious, dangerous, sexy promises of what he would do next into her ear.

Now by a horrible twist of fate, she had become someone's *real* slave, taken by force, locked in a compound and surrounded by dangerous men who, she sincerely believed, would kill her in a heartbeat if she got out of line. Or, more likely, they would sell her ass for sex, and she'd end up dead after a year from some horrible sexually transmitted disease.

Spurred on by the desire to avoid these potential fates, Leah made herself concentrate on the task at hand. At least the man was clean and not too hairy. His cock was smooth, the skin silky over the steel of his erection. Licking the sweet spot just below the head of his cock, she stroked his balls with one hand and gripped the base of the long shaft with the other. She felt his hand on the back of her head, pressing gently. Taking the hint, she lowered herself farther onto the shaft, trying to relax enough to take it into her throat as he'd commanded.

He moaned softly and pressed a little harder against her head, gagging her with the sudden movement. She struggled to stay calm and open her throat. He gripped a handful of her hair, twining it tightly around his fingers. He muttered something in Arabic and grunted, thrusting against her mouth while she tried to maintain her position.

She willed herself to ease into what she called *the zone*, letting her mind empty as her body took over. The man had considerable staying power and was probably holding off as long as he could to prolong the pleasure. Leah redoubled her efforts, licking, sucking and massaging his shaft with every ounce of skill she possessed, all the while stroking and fondling his heavy balls.

She felt him tense and a shudder moved through his body. "*Y'allah!*" he shouted as he climaxed, his jism nearly choking her as it shot down her throat. Pulling his wet cock from her lips, he fell back against the chair with a contented sigh.

Leah let her hands fall away and knelt back on her haunches, not sure what was expected of her now. She stayed quiet and still, even resisting the desire to wipe her mouth with the back of her hand, not willing to find out if this was permitted or not.

The naked man remained sprawled against the chair with complete, unselfconscious abandon while Leah knelt before him, feeling both fearful and a little triumphant that she'd made the bastard come. Finally he deigned to open his eyes, focusing slowly on Leah, his mouth curling into a lazy, contented smile.

"You did well, little one. You have pleased me." He clapped his hands three times in rapid succession, startling Leah. A young woman who barely looked to be out of her teens appeared suddenly from a side door Leah hadn't noticed before. She had long, thick dark hair that fell in shimmering waves down her back. She was dressed in a series of veils that revealed as much as they hid. She sank gracefully down, forehead to the ground, hands extended as Leah had been taught earlier by the steward.

He said something in rapid Arabic to the girl. She rose fluidly, her eyes downcast, replying in a soft, sweet voice in the same language. When the girl disappeared again, Khalil turned to Leah.

"Naeemah will have the cook prepare you a small meal. I personally will feed you." He said this as if she should be overcome with awe and gratitude at such a privilege. Still, she was very hungry, the three tiny sandwiches and wedge of baklava only a memory.

Taking a deep breath, she replied, "Thank you, Master," the appellation forced from her lips by a sheer act of will, made easier by the promise of food.

Khalil left Leah kneeling on the small rug while he moved around the room. Her knees were aching by the time the food arrived. Khalil had pulled on a pair of dark blue silk lounge pants, leaving his chest bare. A low table that held several covered dishes was wheeled into the room by a male servant, bringing with it heavenly aromas of cardamom, cinnamon and roasted lamb. He lifted the lids from the dishes, revealing a steaming bowl of yellow rice with chunks of potato, carrot and peas and a plate with five small skewers of grilled shish kebab. There was a bottle of white wine beside the food, a single glass beside it. Leah's mouth was watering and she swallowed hard as she stared at the feast.

She almost didn't mind being fed, and forgot the pain in her knees as Khalil spooned the flavorful rice into her mouth or offered a morsel of the tender, spicy lamb. She chewed quickly, eager for each offered bite, grateful for the sustenance. Unlike her previous experiences since the abduction, she wasn't denied food after a few mouthfuls. Khalil allowed her to eat her fill, alternating bites of food with the wine, a fruity chardonnay.

She was actually full when he'd emptied the platters, and a little drunk from the two glasses of wine.

She felt almost grateful to the man who purchased human beings for his own amusement. Almost.

Leaning down, Khalil removed her barrettes. He stroked her cheek and tucked her hair behind her ears, smiling at her as if they were lovers. She stifled the urge to scream, praying her face didn't betray her fury. "You will sleep at my feet tonight, little one." Leah wasn't sure if he meant on the floor of his bedroom or literally at his feet on the huge, high bed, but figured she'd find out soon enough.

He allowed her to use the bathroom in private and even provided her with a new toothbrush. When she emerged, having stayed in the bathroom as long as she dared, Khalil was sitting on the edge of the huge canopied bed. He'd turned off the overhead light and the room was lit by a stained glass lamp that stood on a small table inlaid with mother of pearl beside the bed.

He beckoned to her with a crooked finger. Leah approached hesitantly, still not sure if she was supposed to lie down on the floor or the bed. "Come closer, little one. Do not be shy." He swung his legs from the bed and stood, naked again, his cock at half mast. He pointed to the end of the mattress and Leah saw the chain wrapped around one of the posts with several metal clips attached.

"Lie down and put your wrists together. The chain is long and will allow you to move as you sleep." He smiled again and lifted his chin, as if waiting for her to thank him for the great gift of a long chain. To cover her bases, Leah forced herself to thank him, supposing she should be grateful. Sleeping on the bed was definitely better than being shoved beneath the stairs or thrown in a dog kennel. She would rather have been left to her own devices in the room she'd been taken to after her bath, but apparently she'd done such a good job sucking the dickwad's cock that she had earned the *privilege* of sleeping with his feet in her face.

She did as she was told, lying down on the soft sheets and holding her wrists obediently together while he clipped the O rings to the chain. There was enough play in the chain to allow her to move, though she was pretty much limited to lying on her side. Khalil placed a light coverlet over her body. Leah would have liked a pillow, but didn't dare ask.

She almost sighed aloud with relief to realize she'd made it through the day alive and relatively intact. She was exhausted and couldn't wait to escape the terror of this ongoing ordeal for at least a few hours. The healing peace of a good night's sleep would hopefully give her courage to face whatever lay ahead.

Khalil climbed into bed above her and with a flick of the lamp, the room was plunged into darkness, save for the silvery glow of the rising moon outside the window. Leah's eyelids were heavy, aided by her full stomach and the wine. She let them close and tucked her hands beneath her head for a pillow, the chains clanking as she moved.

Khalil's next words made her eyes fly open and set her heart pounding. "By the way, I am especially fond of nipple torture. I am curious to see how long you can last, little one. My most accomplished slave girl endured more than thirty minutes before she could take no more. In the morning we will take your measure and see how you compare."

Any hope of sleep had vanished. Long after Khalil had begun to snore, Leah lay rigid and wide-eyed, staring at the moon until it disappeared from view.

Chapter 8

Devin ran his fingers through his hair and stretched his neck with a groan. He'd been at it for hours. The papers from George's files were spread all over the desk, with more fanning out on the floor beside him. He had nearly used up the packet of index cards he'd purchased for the purpose, filling them with notes from the files.

He stared again at the dozen or so photos of various properties that George had rounded up when trying to pinpoint the location of the slave compound. From his own work in real estate, Devin was familiar with several of the properties owned by Asian and European millionaires whom he doubted had anything to do with slave trafficking. There were gorgeous villas, built on beautifully landscaped terraced cliffs overlooking the ocean. An aerial view of one sprawling property included a garden filled with life-size sculptures of wild horses that appeared to be carved from marble. Another boasted a pool terrace with a glass-bottomed infinity pool that spilled over into the sea.

Devin had what he hoped were several promising leads to pursue, but he needed to organize his thoughts better and figure out a strategic plan of attack. His head ached and there was a dull pain in his stomach he realized was from hunger. In his single-minded focus on

George's files, he'd completely forgotten about food. In fact, he realized he hadn't eaten anything since Leah had gone missing the day before.

Devin knew he should get some dinner, though he didn't have much of an appetite, despite his hunger. Still, he wouldn't be much help to Leah if he didn't keep up his strength, and so he reached for the room phone. "This is Mr. Lyons in room 1404. Please send up a steak, rare, and some chips. Oh, and a bottle of Guinness."

While waiting for his meal, Devin organized his index cards into piles—one pile with the names and information on the people George had interviewed in relation to the abductions, one pile with what little information there was about the compound that was the suspected hub of the slave trade, and one pile about sex trafficking in general, and the Thai sex industry in particular.

Devin looked at his watch. It was nearly eight o'clock, and the exotic dance and strip clubs would be opening for the evening. As soon as he ate and showered, he would go to Pattaya's red light district, the neon-drenched strip known as Walking Street, which stretched from Soi 13 to 16. In reviewing George's notes, he'd found the information about the Thai girl who had been abducted but then released. According to the notes, she worked at Happy GoGo Club. Devin had his fingers crossed that she was still there.

Room service arrived and Devin forced himself to eat, though he barely tasted the food. As he ate, his mind drifted over the one perfect night he had shared with Leah. As he thought of the lovely woman he'd left sleeping like an angel in his bed, the unwelcome thought that he might never see her again slithered into his brain like a snake. Even if he found out what happened to her, it might already be too late.

"No!" he shouted, refusing to let his thoughts move to their inevitable conclusion. "Hang on, Leah. Just hang on. I'm coming to find you."

The Happy GoGo Club was dimly lit, except for the spotlights trained on naked girls gyrating on the elevated stage that stretched along the center of the room. Pulsing disco music pumped through the smoke-filled air. Chairs lined the perimeter of the stage, most of them occupied by men who watched the girls with expressions ranging from open-mouthed admiration to world-weary boredom.

Devin made his way to the bar at the back of the room. The bartender was Thai, with longish, greasy hair slicked back from his face. Devin ordered a beer. As the bartender set it before him, Devin put some baht on the bar. "Keep the change."

Palming the money, the bartender asked, "You want lap dance?" He pointed toward the section of the room that contained freestanding tables, a few of which were occupied by men with naked or nearly naked women sitting on their laps. "You pay me. Girls get the tips."

"Actually, I'm looking for a particular girl. Her name is Jaidee. She goes by the name of Lotus Flower." Jaidee was his best hope for pinpointing the actual location of the compound. Assuming Leah was even there. Devin knew his theory was crammed with way too many assumptions, but what else did he have to go on?

The bartender eyed Devin suspiciously. "No Lotus Flower here. You want lap dance? I got lots of girls, best in Pattaya."

"I'm looking for Jaidee. I just want to talk to her."

The bartender shook his head. "She no here. No more. I got better girls. Much prettier girls." He cupped his hands at his chest to indicate gargantuan breasts. "My girls know what a man wants." He winked.

Devin put his hands on the bar, leaning forward. "I don't want a lap dance. I'm looking for Jaidee Anantasu."

"I tell you. She no here." The bartender started to turn away, a scowl on his face.

Devin reached again into his pocket, withdrawing a wad of baht, which he slapped onto the bar. Forcing himself to speak politely, he said, "Perhaps you have some information that would help me track her down. I would greatly appreciate it."

The bartender turned slowly back, his eyes on the money. "She quit two months ago. How I know where she go? I don't own these girls." He placed his hand over the money and looked at Devin, the scowl now replaced with a smile.

"Maybe you could give it some thought. It's a matter of the utmost importance. Any help you can offer would be most appreciated." Devin waited. The man, his hand still on the money, regarded Devin with raised eyebrows.

"I think I might remember," he said slowly. "It's been a while though."

"Perhaps I can help jog your memory." Devin slid another packet of Thai money across the bar, praying the man had the information he was desperately seeking.

The bartender put his other hand over the second pile of cash and slid both from the bar. "I have maybe something. No promises." He moved toward the cash register. Reaching beneath the counter, he pulled out what looked like a small, black leather address book, stuffed with loose pieces of paper. Opening it on the counter, he riffled through the pages until he found what he was looking for. Taking one of the scraps of paper, he pulled a plastic pen from his shirt pocket, crossed out whatever was on the scrap and scribbled something beneath it.

Looking at Devin, he slid the piece of paper across the bar. "Last I hear, she at The Blue Dream. Vastly inferior club, over on Second Road. My girls better. You stay for lap dance, eh? No charge."

"Another time." Devin took the scrap of paper on which the bartender had written the address of the rival club, clutching it like a lifeline.

~*~

Devin felt as if he were in a kind of surreal nightmare, with this scantily clad girl wiggling on his lap while Leah might already be dead. He'd been at The Blue Dream for nearly an hour waiting for his turn with Jaidee, who was apparently quite popular.

It was awkward trying to interview the girl from this position, but she'd refused to sit at the table, darting glances in the direction of the bartender, whom Devin suspected was also her pimp. "I dance for you, yes? Make you happy."

She was a pretty girl, with high cheekbones, large, dark almond-shaped eyes and a pouty little mouth. Devin had been trying for ten minutes to tease any information out of her about her abduction experience, but she either didn't understand or refused to discuss it. Finally she put a long-nailed finger over his lips. "You want talk, we go to back room for naughty play. Fifteen hundred baht, cheap! I talk dirty to you, yes? You like that?"

She placed a small hand over Devin's crotch. Devin stood, lifting the girl in the process and setting her on her feet. "Okay, fine. Let's go to a back room." He tried to keep the frustration from his voice, aware she was only doing her job.

With a wide smile and another surreptitious glance at the bartender, Jaidee held her hand out to Devin, who took it. She led him through a door that opened onto a narrow hallway with doors along one wall, each painted a different color. She stopped in front of the red door. The small room was decorated rather as Devin had expected, most of the space taken up by a bed, the lamp beside it covered with a red lampshade that cast the room in a pinkish glow. There was a small, rickety looking bureau, over which hung a large mirror that faced the bed.

The girl stood smiling politely, her head tilted as she regarded him. "You please to put the cash there." She pointed to the bureau. Devin pulled out his wallet, thinking briefly how much he'd spent so far in what he prayed wasn't a fool's errand. He set the bills on the bureau.

Devin sat on the bed, suddenly realizing how exhausted he was. He ran his hands through his hair and over his face. His eyes felt gritty and he wanted to take a hot shower and climb into bed, but he knew he wouldn't rest until he'd found Leah.

Jaidee slid the spaghetti straps of her flimsy sundress from her shoulders. "No, that's okay," Devin said, holding out a hand with its palm toward her. "I told you before—I just want to talk to you. I need some information."

Jaidee moved close to him. She smelled of sweat and cheap perfume. "You want I talk dirty to get you in the mood? Tell you the naughty things I will do to you? Yes, yes. I understand." She shimmied the slinky dress from her slender body and cupped her small breasts in her hands, leaning forward in what she must have thought was a provocative pose. She looked so young, with her narrow hips and tiny breasts, though Devin realized she was probably older than she appeared. Watching her, he felt more embarrassed than attracted.

"Please," he tried again, making his tone firm. "Put your dress back on, Jaidee." He pointed to the dress puddled on the floor, waiting until she bent down to retrieve it. Reluctantly she pulled it over her head, her mouth turned down in a pout.

She crossed her arms, the pout edging into a worried glare. "No money back. You come in room, you pay. End of story, Mister."

"Absolutely. I understand, Jaidee. The money is yours. And a nice tip, too, if you can help me with what I need. Please," he tried again, patting the bed beside him. "Come sit down. I want to ask you some questions. I'm trying to find someone. Someone very close to me. You might be able to help me. Please, Jaidee, I need your help."

Jaidee looked incredulous. "You don't want naughty play?" Again her small mouth turned into a downward pout and she put her hands on her hips. "My tits not big enough for American man?"

Devin shook his head, a small, exasperated laugh erupting from his lips. "I'm British, not American. And believe me, you're lovely, Jaidee. If I wanted naughty play, you would be the one I chose. But what I need from you now is your help. A woman's life may well hang in the balance."

Looking somewhat mollified, Jaidee finally came to sit beside him on the bed. Satisfied he had her full attention at last, Devin said, "I'm looking for a woman I believe has been abducted." When the girl looked blank, he added, "kidnapped, taken by bad men."

Jaidee's eyes widened and she nodded, though her face had become guarded. Determined, Devin continued, "I know from my investigations you were taken by bad men last year — taken to a place where this woman might be now. I need to know anything you can tell me about it."

Turning away from Devin, Jaidee wrapped her thin arms around her torso and leaned forward, her hair falling in a dark, shiny curtain over her face. "Please," Devin said quietly, putting a hand on her shoulder.

When Jaidee looked back at him, all trace of coquettishness was gone and she suddenly looked her age, which he guessed was closer to thirty than twenty. "I was lucky I get free," she said. "I have friends, men who take care of me. They get me out."

Devin wondered just how well these men "took care" of Jaidee, putting her to work as a prostitute, but of course he said nothing, waiting for her to continue. Jaidee shook her hair back, meeting his eye. "I no want to talk on this. Bad luck."

He tried to keep his voice calm, though he wanted to shake her. "I understand, Jaidee. It must be hard to talk about. But I need to find the place. It will be very bad luck for my friend if I don't find her."

Reaching again for his wallet, he withdrew more bills, placing them on Jaidee's thigh. As she put her hand over the money, he said, "I need you to tell me any details you can remember. Something particular or unusual about where you were kept that might help me pinpoint the location."

The girl sucked on her finger and regarded the ceiling. "Big rooms. Very fancy. Like a palace. I not there long. Lucky me, I not what the big man looking for." She grimaced. "They take me away, make me lie down in back, my eyes covered with cloth. But they don't do the cloth tight. I could see little bit from underneath, like so." Jaidee demonstrated, tilting her chin upward and looking down her nose. "I saw the ocean. And I saw white horses, so pretty."

"Horses?" Devin grabbed onto the words, something triggering in his memory.

"How you say—statues? They were very beautiful, made all in stone. White stone."

Excitement gripped Devin as he thought back over the photos of the various locations George had collected in his investigation. What were the odds there was more than one wild horse sculpture garden along the Thai coast? Devin's heart began to thud. Finally something concrete to hold onto.

Had George known what he had? Devin recalled the investigator's comment: *I got really close, but I got shut down by officials who didn't want me to succeed for reasons of their own.* And if Jaidee had been able to identify the location, didn't that put her in danger as well, as someone who knew too much?

"Jaidee, did you tell anyone else about the horses?"

The girl shook her head.

"Why not?"

Jaidee shrugged. "No one ask."

Chapter 9

"Devin, my boy. I thought you were in Thailand. Is everything okay?"

"I am in Thailand. And no, everything's not okay. That's why I'm calling. I need your help."

Uncle Ron had been more like a father than an uncle to Devin, stepping in to help Devin's mother after his father had been killed in a car accident when Devin was twelve. Devin sorely hoped his uncle could help now. He was Sir Ronald Lyons, Superintendent at Scotland Yard, with extensive experience in Asian affairs and ties to Interpol, the international police.

Devin began to pour out the story, trying to keep his voice steady as he related the events that had unfolded over the past couple of days.

"What time is it there? It's late, no?" Uncle Ron asked.

"A little after midnight. I just came from a club where I spoke with a Thai woman who was taken briefly to the compound where I think Leah might be." He filled in his uncle on the details of his talk with Jaidee.

"Where are you calling from now?" There was an urgency to Uncle Ron's tone that unsettled Devin.

"I'm on my mobile. I'm back at my hotel."

"Okay, good. Don't use any landlines, and don't talk about this to any of the local authorities. Who have you gone to so far besides this PI of yours?"

"I went to the police when Leah first went missing yesterday evening, but they wouldn't do anything about it. The concierge at the hotel claimed she checked out and went on to Bangkok, but I know he's lying. He's got to be in on whatever is going on. She's not the first to disappear—"

"Hold on, will you? I need to look something up. I have to boot my computer." Devin, who had been pacing the room, went over to the bed and sat down heavily. Every muscle and bone in his body ached, but at the same time he felt hopeful. His uncle hadn't dismissed his story, but seemed to be taking it seriously—very seriously.

After a few minutes, Uncle Ron was back on the line. "Devin, listen to me. It's worse than I feared. You've stumbled into something quite dangerous. Interpol is working with the Royal Thai Police. They've created a special task force and they're getting close to a bust. You need to be very careful. They're aware that an American citizen was recently reported missing. But this is bigger than just some American woman being abducted."

"It's not just some woman, Uncle Ron. She's—I'm—we—" Though he was alone in the room, Devin felt his face heating.

"You've got it bad, huh?" His uncle laughed and Devin could almost see his craggy, kind face. The laughter eased the tight knot in Devin's stomach, just a little.

"Yeah," he admitted. "I never believed in that love at first sight nonsense but—"

"Why ever not?" his uncle interrupted. "When I first saw your Aunt Mirabel my freshman year at Oxford, sitting pretty as you please beneath that old oak tree near the commons, it was all over. Here we are forty-two years later, and I've never looked back."

Devin smiled in spite of himself, having heard the story of his aunt and uncle's first meeting a dozen times over the years. The fact that Aunt Mirabel had been engaged at the time to another man hadn't fazed Uncle Ron in the slightest.

Recalling himself, Devin persisted. "I need your help, Uncle Ron. I need to be a part of this. I have to find Leah."

"Understood. Fax me those files you obtained, and the photos of the property. I'll coordinate with my contacts at Interpol and see if they can't use you somehow. Your position with the estate agency might provide just the cover they need to gain access. But Devin, we're not going to get much done until the sun comes up over there. It's six o'clock in the evening here, but I'll see what I can find out on this end, and give you a call first thing in the morning, Thai time. Meanwhile, get some rest, will you? You sound beat."

"Yeah," Devin agreed, rubbing at the grit in his eyes. "Thank you, Uncle Ron. I owe you big time."

"You owe me nothing, nephew. Now get some rest. Good night."

"'Night. And thanks."

Devin let himself fall back against the pillows, too exhausted suddenly even to take off his clothing. Closing his eyes, he felt himself being sucked down into a deep, dreamless sleep.

~*~

Leah found herself bound to a rack that was like something out of a science fiction movie. Made from some kind of metal tubing, it consisted of a circle large enough for a person to stand or lie inside, arms and legs spread in a human X. She was secured at the wrists, ankles and waist, her back supported by a bar that extended across the diameter of the circle. The rack was mounted on a pivot, enabling it to be tilted at any angle, from fully upright to completely horizontal.

At the moment, Leah was upright, staring at an image of herself in a mirror that covered an entire wall. The room, like the torture chamber the steward had taken her to, contained BDSM equipment and gear, but unlike that windowless room, which had the stark, institutional feel of a prison cell, this room had thick pile carpet on the floor, woven tapestries hung along the walls that weren't mirrored, and a queen size bed in one corner, piled with plump pillows and covered with another elaborately woven tapestry. A crystal vase filled with fresh flowers stood on a marble table in front of a large bay window. Sunlight streamed incongruously into the room, gilding the flowers in gold.

Leah had been awakened from a deep sleep that morning by Alex gently shaking her shoulder. Khalil had been nowhere in sight. "Wake up, girl. The Master will see you in an hour. We have to get you groomed and ready."

Just behind Alex stood one of the guards, burly arms crossed over his barrel chest, his eyes dead as stones. She was permitted to drink some water, but other than that nothing was offered, and though she'd eaten well the night before, she was starving.

While Alex groomed and prepared Leah, Khalil's threat of nipple torture from the night before loomed heavy in her mind. She tried to engage Alex in a whispered conversation about what was in store for her, but he ignored her completely, never making eye contact as he bathed and shaved her and applied another round of the full makeup.

When Alex was satisfied, he rang a small bell he took out of his sleeve. After a moment, the second guard joined the first and she was escorted, none too gently, to this mirrored, over-decorated BDSM dungeon. After they strapped her to the circular rack, the guards withdrew, closing the door silently behind them.

Leah looked away from the mirror, hating the sight of herself with shaven pussy and rouged nipples, her painted face painted like that of a stranger. She jumped when the door opened. Khalil entered, again decked out in his white silk shirt and lounge pants, his feet bare.

He stopped just inside the door, insolently raking her naked, spread eagle body for several long moments, his hand moving to massage his rising cock beneath the silk. Moving closer, he asked, "Sleep well, little one? You were like an angel when I woke, your hair spread over the sheets like hammered gold. I have chosen well to honor you with my attention. I know you're eager to prove your worth this morning, so I won't keep you waiting any longer."

Leah said nothing, though his words, said with such self-assured arrogance, sent a chill of pure terror down her spine. The man was clearly insane. Did he really delude himself that she was eager to prove anything, or somehow *honored* to be kidnapped and brutalized?

Khalil went to an ornate black cabinet and pulled open a drawer. He returned to Leah with a pair of clover clamps. Leah was no stranger to that type of clamp, and even owned her own pair for playing BDSM games. She loved the intensity as her nipples were caught in the tight grip of the clamps, especially when her lover would lick and tease her compressed, engorged nipples while gently tugging on the chain. The heady blend of pleasure and pain had always thrilled her, tapping in to her core passion for erotic suffering.

But there was nothing erotic about what was happening now. The thought of Khalil using the clamps on her nipples made Leah sick with fear. She knew he would follow no safe or sane rules in his sadistic pursuits. Safewords didn't exist in his vocabulary. He'd made that clear enough the night before.

She shut her eyes as he tugged at her nipples and closed the clamps over each. He gave the chain a savage tug, drawing a scream from Leah.

"You can do better than that, surely? I have such hopes for you."

He stepped away, returning with a flogger. "Forgive me. I moved too quickly in my eagerness to test you. I didn't tell you the rules. I am going to warm your skin first with this flogger and help put you in a better mindset for what I have planned."

He stroked her breasts with the leather tresses, dragging them heavily over her clamped nipples. Her nipples were throbbing but she knew from experience they would soon numb to the point where she could deal with the pain.

"Here is what I expect." Khalil said, as he struck her breasts, stomach and thighs with the flogger. "Whatever I do to you, no matter how much it hurts, I expect you to stay utterly silent. I understand this will be difficult at times, and while I wish for perfection, I know you are limited, untrained as you are. Just be aware, the more unseemly yelping and cries that fall from those pretty lips, the harsher shall be your punishment at the hands of the guards when we are through."

He dragged the flogger down her body and ran it between her legs, using both hands to pull it hard against her spread cunt. Leah tried not to wince and after a few seconds he let it fall. Leaning in close, he said softly, "If you displease me, I shall instruct them to beat you until they draw blood."

Leah began to tremble, unable to stop her body from registering her terror or prevent the small whimper that escaped her lips. She thought of Setsuko locked in that punishment cage, her back welted and bloodied, and knew Khalil would make good on his threat.

"There, there, little one," Khalil said softly, stroking her cheek. "Your fear is exciting to me, but I still demand your obedience. I have great faith in your potential. Stay silent and take what I give you with the grace of a true slave girl. For while the punishment if you fail will be swift and harsh, so shall the reward be great. The longer you stay silent, the more you will please me. I know that is what you crave, what all my girls crave, which is as it should be."

Leah took a deep breath. Somehow she had to get through this. While she hated the idea of doing anything to please this insane megalomaniac, she recognized it was better to please than displease him. He had complete control and all the power. The only thing she could exercise was her will.

Lifting the chain, he tugged again at her nipples. As she'd hoped, they had numbed to the point where she could tolerate the pain. She closed her eyes, trying to let her mind empty.

You can do this. You can do this. You can do this.

Her eyes flew open when he tilted the rack, moving her to a horizontal position. For a moment she felt as if she were falling, but she was securely tethered to the rack. She couldn't move an inch. Khalil lifted the chain between the clamps, pulling it up, reawakening her numbed nerve endings in the process. Leah drew in a sharp breath, but somehow managed to stay silent.

Reaching into his pants pocket, Khalil withdrew a two-sided clip, attaching one side to the center of the chain, and the other to the O ring on Leah's slave collar. The tension increased on Leah's tortured nipples, but she pressed her lips together, refusing to let a single sound escape.

Leaving her a moment, Khalil returned with a short-handled, single tail whip. He snapped it against her right breast, the tip catching painfully against the underside. Leah couldn't help the gasp that slipped past her lips. Her heart was beating like a drum.

He struck the other breast, leaving a matching line of fire. Tears smarted behind Leah's eyelids but she blinked them rapidly back, refusing to cry in front of her tormentor. He continued to flick the whip, almost casually, the strokes seemingly random, though each flick was harder than the last.

When the whip caught her left nipple dead on, Leah lost control and cried out. Khalil frowned. "And you were doing so well, little one." He shrugged, adding, "Ah well. No matter. We will try something new."

Without warning, he reached for the clamps and released them from her nipples. Leah opened her mouth in a silent scream of pure agony as the blood rushed back into her tortured nipples, but by some miracle, she managed to stay quiet.

Khalil smiled and nodded. "Good girl. Much better." After releasing the chain from her collar, he pushed at the side of the rack, lifting her upright again. Moving toward the cabinet, he returned with something that looked positively medieval. They appeared to be another type of nipple clamps, but instead of padded tips, the ends were comprised of tiny spiked teeth.

Leah instinctively tried to shrink back as Khalil moved closer, pressing one of the clamps open as he grabbed her right nipple and pulled it taut. She closed her eyes, turning her head away as the sharp metal teeth bit into her flesh. When he attached the second one, she made the mistake of looking down. At the sight of the droplets of bright red blood circling her clamped nipples, she felt sick and rapidly looked away.

Again she encouraged herself with the silent words: *You can do this. You can do this.* Her nipples stung and throbbed, but the pain wasn't intolerable. But Khalil wasn't done. He attached heavy lead weights to the chain that dangled between the vicious clamps. As the weight tugged at the teeth, they sank deeper into Leah's skin. Keeping her eyes closed, Leah began to count slowly, trying to match her breathing to the numbers.

One...two...three...four...five...

"Yes," Khalil said in an excited voice. "Beautiful. The red blood against the white skin. Flowers in the virgin snow."

...six...seven...eight...nine...

Leah felt herself being tilted again. She felt Khalil's hard thighs pressing between hers and lost track of the counting as her eyes involuntarily flew open. He'd pulled off his shirt and his pants were around his knees, his erect cock in his hand.

Desperately Leah tried to close her legs, but she couldn't move at all. Khalil hovered over her, his shaft near her spread pussy, which she was certain was dry as a bone. *No, no, no, no,* she prayed silently, her tortured nipples almost forgotten at the prospect of being raped by this bastard.

But instead of plunging into her, he moved closer, leaning over her stomach. He was tugging and jerking at his cock with one hand, while he reached for Leah's breasts with the other. He drew a circle around one of her clamped nipples and then moved the finger over her lips, leaving them wet with, Leah realized with horror, her own blood.

Letting go of his cock, he reached with both hands for Leah's breasts, releasing the biting clamps from her nipples and tossing the weighted chain aside. Leah couldn't help herself. She began to cry as much from mental exhaustion as pain.

"There, there," Khalil cooed. "Don't cry. You should be proud. You have earned your reward. One day, if you merit it, I might even give you the honor of my cock inside your worthless female body. Would that please you?"

"Yes, Master," Leah lied, hating him as she'd never hated another human being.

Khalil nodded and smiled, showing those white, perfect teeth, his pink tongue sliding over his lips as he grabbed his cock again and began to pump it. It wasn't long before he was panting and grunting, his hand moving over his shaft in a frenzy.

Do it. Do it, you motherfucker. Come and then get the hell away from me.

As if responding to her silent order, Khalil began to shudder. He stiffened and then jerked forward, shooting his warm, gooey come over her stomach and breasts with a loud groan. He leaned heavily against her and she could feel his heart beating. His chest was slick with sweat, and the salt stung her torn skin.

Eventually he lifted himself from her, staring down at her with his dark, liquid eyes. "I am pleased with you, little one. You have exceeded my expectations. While it is true you will require a great deal of training to reach your full potential, I can forgive much because of your blond perfection. I find I simply must have you for my harem." His eyes narrowed, glinting with cruelty. "Don't make me regret my decision to bestow this honor upon you."

Leah had no idea if she was expected to respond to this madman. What he was saying made no sense to her.

All she knew was that her nipples hurt like hell. She was thirsty, hungry, and covered in this bastard's sweat and spunk and her own blood. She just wanted to be let down. She wanted him to go away. She wanted to wash the filth from her body. She wanted to sleep.

She was relieved when he released her cuffs and waist restraint. She would have fallen but he caught her easily in his arms and carried her to the bed in the corner of the room. Laying her gently on the soft sheets, he said, "Rest for a while, little one. Alex will bathe you and you shall eat. And after that, your reward."

Leah wondered what this reward might be. Sleeping *beside* the great *Master* instead of at his feet? Having the *privilege* of him rutting inside her like a pig? Getting to kneel at his feet like a dog so he could force feed her a meal? Was she really expected to be *grateful* to this bastard?

What he said next made all other thoughts vanish in a flash of pure terror.

"I will bestow my mark of permanent ownership upon you. The branding will take place tonight."

Chapter 10

Leah winced as Alex brushed rouge over her nipples. Though she'd been permitted to soak in a hot tub of oil-scented water after the torture on the rack, her breasts were still sore and tender to the touch. She was being dressed, if it could be called that, in thin chains that fit over her body like a bra and hip belt, outlining her naked form in glinting silver.

She'd been allowed to eat her fill of a delicious meal including fresh fruit, cheese, bread, three kinds of olives and more of the wonderful baklava, but she'd barely tasted the food, her mind still reeling from Khalil's threat.

Branded!

Somehow she had to stop this, but had no idea how. She drank three glasses of the strong wine that accompanied the meal, its sweet burn blunting the worst of her terror. When Leah had been led back to her small bedroom, she'd expected to toss and turn, but had instead fallen into a deep, dreamless sleep, exhausted by the ordeals she'd endured and sedated by the wine.

Now she was being prepared for a ritual that terrified her, not only because of the anticipated pain of having her flesh burned, but the finality of it. Any hope of rescue, by Devin or anyone else, was fast receding.

She was powerless, trapped in a situation from which she could see no escape. The brand would mark her forever as a slave, the property of another human being.

The idea was so absurd on its face that Leah found she couldn't get her head around it. And yet Alex, who seemed so peacefully resigned to his slave collar and his mutilation, was proof that slavery was alive and well in the twenty-first century. She glanced at the two guards who stood nearby, arms folded, faces closed. Were they slaves, too, or were they paid for their services?

Alex attached gauzy, flowing material to Leah's hip belt, creating a see-through skirt that came to Leah's ankles, slit at the center all the way to her bellybutton. He led her to the makeup counter and pointed for her to sit on the stool. Once he'd applied his creams and paints to her face, he turned her toward the mirror and began to pin up her hair.

She caught his eye for a second in the mirror and saw the flash of pity in his face before he looked away. "Please, Alex," she whispered, hoping the guards standing near the door couldn't hear her. "What's going to happen to me? I'm so afraid."

Alex shook his head, saying nothing as he placidly continued to pull the glittering bobby pins he held between his lips, using them to create an elaborate chignon at the nape of her neck. When he was done, he surprised her by leaning close, his words a murmur in her ear.

"Be thankful he has chosen you. Be thankful he chooses to let you live."

These words echoed in Leah's mind as she was hustled between the guards to the Master's quarters. What kind of life would this be, branded like cattle, kept in chains, whipped and raped, always wondering if this day would be her last? How long would it take until she completely lost her mind?

Leah was brought into Khalil's bedroom and led through it into a marble bathroom, similar to the one where she was bathed and groomed, but even larger. Khalil was standing at a counter, his back to her. The guards led Leah to a squat wooden chair, its wide padded seat upholstered in wine-red velvet. The guard nodded curtly toward the ground and Leah, recalling the steward's orders, lowered herself to the floor until her forehead touched the cold marble tile, her palms pressed flat in front of her.

After a moment she felt the touch of a hand on her shoulder and then Khalil's smooth, deep voice with its precise diction. "Ah, little one. You may rise and present yourself."

Leah lifted her head. Khalil turned to face her as she forced herself to her feet. The handsome monster offered his beautiful, white smile, sending chills down Leah's spine. "You are so lovely in your chains and gossamer," he said, his liquid eyes burning with a feverish light. "Truly a golden princess, born to serve."

Leah saw Khalil was holding some kind of implement in his hand. He held it by its wooden handle, from which protruded a metal stick that ended in a circle of stainless steel shaped into some kind of pattern. Leah felt a hot rush of horror rip through her body as she realized what she was seeing.

Khalil, watching her, nodded, still smiling. "That's right, little one. This is for you. My personal crest, developed especially to mark my chosen girls. Once I mark you, no man will dare to touch you. You will be forever branded with the mark of Yousef Khalil."

Turning to the guards, he said, "Prepare the slave."

The guards took hold of her on either side. Though Leah knew it was worse than useless, panic twisted through her limbs, making her jerk against the strong fingers circling her upper arms as she tried to wrench herself free.

"No!" she cried, the word bursting from her lips. "No!"

She was no match for the burly men, who easily wrestled her down, forcing her into the chair. Though she continued to struggle, her wrists were bound to the arms of the chair, her ankles secured to the legs of the wide seat, which forced her knees to spread open. Panic gripped her and she could feel her heart squeezing in her chest.

"Please, please! I'm begging you. Don't do this. Please!" she wailed, bursting into tears.

The sharp crack of Khalil's hard palm across her cheek made her gasp with shocked pain. "Stop it at once!" he shouted, glowering at her. "I will not have a girl of mine behaving with such cowardice."

He turned toward the impassive guards. "You may go," he said brusquely.

As they slipped silently out of the room, Khalil knelt in front of Leah, his face softening. "Accept my mark with the courage worthy of a prince's slave. If you continue this disgraceful display, I will have no choice but to have you beaten until you are good for nothing but the lowest rung of whoredom—chained to a cot in the back room of the lowliest brothel."

Leah swallowed hard, fully believing his threat. She tried to gulp down her sobs, though her body continued to shake. She squeezed her eyes shut, conjuring the image of Devin Lyons in her head, as if in the thinking he might somehow suddenly appear, bursting through the door like Indiana Jones to save the girl at the last second from certain and painful death.

But this wasn't the movies, and Devin was only a memory. Leah was alone and at the mercy of a sadistic madman, with no one to rescue her, and no way out.

She winced when he raised his hand again, but this time his touch was gentle on her cheek. "You must be brave. I know you are overwhelmed by such an honor, and offered so quickly. Most girls must be trained for at least a month before I deem them worthy of my brand, no matter their beauty. But you! The way you took the pain today, I could see at once you were destined to serve me."

He stroked her face, tucking a loose tendril of hair behind her ear. "That's better. I don't like when you cry. It ruins your lovely face." He pushed himself to his feet, moving out of Leah's line of sight. She could hear the sound of running water. A moment later he returned, dabbing a cool washcloth over her hot cheeks and burning eyelids.

"I am not a cruel man," he said, which, despite her terror and exhaustion, nearly made Leah laugh. Not a cruel man? Was he really that deluded? Or just plain fucking nuts!

Khalil continued, "I understand you are frightened. Know this—it is quick, and I have done this many times. Afterward you will be proud of wearing my mark, and it will protect you from other men. No one dares to take one of my chosen women."

His hand moved from her cheek, trailing over her breasts. He circled her still-tender nipples with his fingers, lightly touching the tiny scabs caused by the spiked nipple clamps. Lowering his head, he lightly licked and sucked each nipple with the gentleness of a lover. Leah closed her eyes, hating the man with every fiber of her being. He continued to glide his lips down her body, leaving a trail of tiny kisses.

"Your skin is like cream, softer than the finest silk," he murmured, as his mouth moved over her shaven mons. Leah longed to slam her legs together. She had a sudden fantasy of ripping through the ropes with superhuman force, lifting the chair and smashing it over Khalil's head.

She sat immobilized in her bonds as Khalil crouched between her spread knees. When the tip of his tongue touched her sex, Leah jerked, clenching her jaw to keep from screaming. He licked in a circle around her hooded clit and drew his tongue lower, pressing it lightly into her entrance.

He placed his hands on her thighs, spreading her labia with his long fingers as his tongue moved upwards, flicking again at her sweet spot. While his attentions were unwelcome, it was the first thing he'd done to her that hadn't caused pain. His touch was surprisingly sensual, and despite her fear and loathing, his skilled attentions were beginning to have an effect.

As he licked and suckled her sex, he pressed a finger inside her and she gave an involuntary grunt before again pressing her lips together. She would not give this bastard the satisfaction of knowing he was getting to her.

Despite her resistance, Khalil was relentless, teasing her clit with his tongue while finger fucking her until her body began to betray her. She could feel the shuddering rise of a climax. Forgetting her promise to resist his touch, she let herself slide past the fear into the bit of pleasure he offered. As the orgasm washed over her, she clung to its brief, obliterating comfort.

Khalil sat back on his haunches. Leah slit her eyes open just enough to see his self-congratulatory smile. *Prick*.

"That was just a taste of what awaits you, little one, when you obey your master. I don't hold with the traditional ideas of pleasure only for the man. On the nights when I choose to take you into my bed, you will experience the ecstasy of my touch, along with the kiss of my lash." He stood, folding his strong arms across his chest, staring down at her with an imperious expression. "You may thank me."

What choice did she have? Hating herself, but hating him far more, she forced the words from her lips. "Thank you, Master," she managed, swallowing the bile that rose in her throat as she said the words.

"And now, it's time," Khalil said. "You shall bear my mark."

Every muscle in Leah's body stiffened, all the pleasure from the orgasm drained away in an instant. Desperately she tried to prepare herself for what she knew was coming. She didn't know where she was going to be branded. Her skin prickled from shoulder to ankle, electrified with dreaded anticipation. She gripped the arms of the chair so hard she thought they might snap in two.

Returning to the counter, Khalil retrieved the brand and a metal cylinder with a nozzle at its end. As he flicked the nozzle to life, a long blue stream of fire appeared. He stuck the head of the brand into the flame.

Leah watched with frozen horror as it changed from silver to a bright, glowing red.

A strange whistling sound began in her ears, though she could hear Khalil's deep, resonant voice beneath it. "It will be quick, little one, no longer than a second or two. I am skilled in the process, applying the proper heat and pressure to create a brand you will be proud to carry for the rest of your life."

Now, Devin! Now. This is the time to come bursting through the door and shoot this bastard right between the eyes.

The door remained shut, and the whistling in Leah's ears grew louder, as black spots appeared before her eyes. She watched in a kind of fear-induced stupor as Khalil shut off the flame of the propane torch and examined the glowing brand in his hand.

"Perfect," he pronounced. Moving behind Leah, he pressed the red-hot metal against Leah's back, just below her right shoulder. For a moment she felt nothing, and then the fiery sear of blinding pain registered itself with a vengeance, while the stench of burning human flesh filled her nostrils.

The black dots faded to an expanding gray and then pure, empty white as Leah floated away.

~*~

Soft, cool fingers moved lightly over Leah's forehead. The scent of a light floral perfume floated into her nostrils. She opened her eyes. The young woman Khalil had called Naeemah was smiling shyly down at her.

Leah was lying on her stomach in a bed, her cheek resting against a soft pillow. She realized she was back in the small bedroom though she had no memory of being taken there. As she came fully awake, she felt the throbbing pain emanating from her shoulder and twisted onto her side, reaching back to try to touch it.

"*La*," Naeemah said, placing a hand on Leah's wrist to stop her. She said something else in Arabic, her voice sweet and lilting. Though Leah didn't understand the words, she could see the pity and compassion in the girl's face.

"I'm sorry. I don't understand." Leah's voice came out hoarse. She cleared her throat.

Leaning over Leah, the girl slipped a surprisingly strong arm beneath Leah's body, helping her to a sitting position. Pushing Leah gently forward, Naeemah rearranged the pillows, careful not to touch the bandaged wound at Leah's shoulder.

Naeemah poured something from a small blue pitcher into a matching blue glass. Leah took the offered glass, expecting water. Instead she smelled something much stronger. She took a tentative sip. It was a strong, sweet wine, mixed with honey and spices. It felt soothing and warm going down, and Leah was grateful Naeemah let her finish the glass.

Leah twisted back, trying to see the bandaged wound on her shoulder. Naeemah said something, holding out her hand in a gesture Leah interpreted as, "Wait."

Leah leaned back carefully against the pillows, watching as Naeemah let the white silk robe she was wearing slip from her bare shoulders. The girl turned, showing her back to Leah. Naeemah had been branded in the same spot just below her right shoulder. The design, a raised pinkish-white scar against the girl's smooth, olive-toned skin, was of a curved blade with a drop of liquid suspended from its tip. It was, Leah realized, a scimitar.

Naeemah let the robe fall all the way to the floor and turned, facing Leah. She was shaven as Leah was, her slave collar and cuffs gold instead of silver. Her breasts were small and high, the tips rouged to a dusty rose. She wore a thin gold chain low over her hips, with what looked like a diamond set in gold dangling at its center. There was a glint of gold between her legs as well, and Leah realized the girl was pierced there.

Naeemah sat on the edge of Leah's bed and reached for the sheet covering Leah's body. She tugged lightly at it, and at first Leah resisted, confused and embarrassed by what the naked girl was doing.

Leaning forward, Naeemah stroked the hair from Leah's face. Her expression was sweet and without guile. She stroked Leah's left shoulder, murmuring something soft and low in her native language. The wine was having its effect too, smoothing some of the jagged edges of fear that had been a constant since the abduction. Naeemah's touch was so soft and gentle, her voice a sweet, if incomprehensible, lullaby. Leah let her eyes close.

When Naeemah tugged again at the sheets, Leah didn't fight her. She felt the air cool against her bare breasts, and then Naeemah's feather-light touch. Leah kept her eyes closed when she felt the soft flick of Naeemah's tongue against her nipple.

Leah lay still, thinking this young woman's gentle, sensual touch was far preferable to Khalil's insistent groping, and certainly better than being beaten. But when she felt the coverlet slide completely away, leaving the rest of her body exposed, Leah opened her eyes.

"I don't—I'm not—" she began, feeling the color surge into her cheeks.

"Shh," Naeemah said, touching a finger to Leah's lips. "It is good," she added in careful English, surprising Leah into silence. The girl pressed Leah back against the pillows. Leah allowed herself to fall back, settling carefully to avoid contact with her bandaged wound.

Reaching for the pitcher, Naeemah poured a second glass of the strong wine and handed it to Leah. Leah took it, not knowing what else to do. For all she knew, Naeemah was under direct orders to do what she was doing, and wouldn't stop until she'd done what she'd been commanded to do. Lifting her head, Leah drank the wine and set the glass down.

The girl began again, lightly kissing and licking Leah's nipples, her small hands stroking and cupping

Leah's breasts until Leah again let her eyes close, sighing with pleasure she couldn't deny.

This time when the girl moved lower, Leah didn't try to fight her. She stayed still, her eyes closed, even when she felt Naeemah scooting between her legs, insistent hands gently pushing her thighs apart.

Leah jumped a little when she felt Naeemah's soft kitten tongue moving lightly over her bared pussy. The woman clearly wasn't a virgin when it came to girl-girl sex. She stroked Leah's thighs as she kissed and licked in teasing circles around and over Leah's rising clit.

Leah finally let go, surrendering to the sweet pleasure Naeemah offered. She sighed, lifting her hips to meet Naeemah's lapping tongue. She reached for Naeemah's head, twining her fingers in the girl's lustrous, dark hair.

Leah gave a small cry as an orgasm arced through her senses—not the powerful, blinding release she'd experienced with Devin, but more of a sweet, tremulous shudder, moving in concentric circles through her body like ripples on the surface of water disturbed by a skimming stone.

A moment later Naeemah sidled up beside her, molding her small, naked form against Leah's side. She reached for Leah's hand, placing it on her own small breast. Embarrassed, Leah pulled her hand away, shaking her head.

Naeemah frowned, her pretty, dark eyes filling with tears. Leah turned her head away. "I'm sorry," she said softly. "I just can't."

They lay quietly side by side for a few minutes. Finally Naeemah whispered something in English it took a moment for Leah to process. Then the girl rolled from the bed and, inexplicably, lowered herself into the slave's greeting position, extending her hands over her head, her forehead pressed to the ground.

Alarmed, Leah swung her head to the corner of the room toward which Naeemah bowed, but no one was there. Naeemah remained in that position for several long seconds before rising in a fluid, graceful motion, retrieving her robe from the floor as she rose. She gave Leah a last reproachful glance and then glanced again to the corner, before slipping through the side door and closing it with a click.

Leah lay still a long moment, Naeemah's unwelcome but not unsurprising words echoing in her head. She reached for the coverlet, drawing it to her chin as she stared at the empty space Naeemah had bowed to. Leah saw nothing at first, but as her eye moved upward she gave a violent start, clutching the sheets in a white-knuckled grip.

There, mounted discreetly where the wall met the ceiling, was a small video camera. Beneath the red blinking light, the lens was aimed at her like a lidless eye, violating Leah with its relentless stare.

She replayed the words Naeemah had whispered in her careful, memorized English before rolling into that servile bow on the floor.

"For the Master," Naeemah had said.

"Fuck the Master," Leah muttered, turning on her side. She reached for the pitcher Naeemah had left behind, but it was empty. Curling into herself, she winced as her bandaged shoulder made contact with the bed. Any lingering pleasure from the orgasm had evaporated, and the constant fear that colored every waking moment since the ordeal had begun had returned in full force.

As Leah lay there, drifting in and out of troubled sleep, all at once, the image of Devin Lyons slipped into her mind, rising from the secret, safe place where she'd tucked him. Did he know she'd been abducted? Was he even now looking for her?

He had to know she wouldn't just vanish without telling him why, or at least goodbye. What they'd shared had been precious, and *real*, so real. He *had* to know something had happened.

Though she didn't believe in such things, or hadn't known she did until that moment, Leah closed her eyes, focusing every bit of her being, from the very depths of her soul, on somehow reaching across the void of time and space, desperate to connect with the one man who might save her.

"Devin," she whispered. "Please find me. Please don't give up."

Though she knew it must be her imagination, Leah felt something move over her—a touch, a whispered promise, a brief, bright light that for that one moment at least blotted out the ever-present fear and gave her the thing she needed most to hang on—hope.

Chapter 11

Devin tugged on the collar of his starched shirt and blew out a breath. Though he'd barely slept the night before, he felt wired and jittery, helped in part by the five cups of coffee he'd had so far that morning. Though the elegant Bentley was air-conditioned, he could feel the sweat dampening the back of his shirt.

The suit he wore was his, but the Italian loafers, hand-sewn silk tie and the emerald and gold cufflinks were not. They had been provided courtesy of the task force, along with the hand-tooled leather portfolio he carried with *Cromwell Estate Agency* stamped in gold lettering on its face, the purchase contract neatly folded inside it.

The briefcase beside him contained more British pounds sterling than he earned in a typical year; again, none of it his. Also in the briefcase were the specs for the property, which Devin had studied exhaustively the day before, working with the task force experts to design a purchase contract that would be hard to turn down, even if the owner claimed he didn't want to sell.

Uncle Ron had come through with flying colors, pulling strings and using his influence with Scotland Yard and Interpol to secure Devin a position with the task force as part of the two-man front team. Though he'd wanted to leap into a car and head immediately for the compound, Interpol hadn't been quite ready for the operation to go forward. They'd spent the day with Devin, briefing him on his role, and refining their own plan of attack. Interpol's goal was to gain legitimate access to the estate.

Now finally, on the fourth day since Leah had gone missing, they were taking some concrete action. The operation, of course, wasn't without risk. They were dealing with criminals, and Devin had been made to understand that if the cover was blown, his life could well be at risk. It was a risk he was more than willing to take if it meant saving the woman who had burst into his life like flashing golden sunshine, and then disappeared without a trace.

Amir Haddad, a fifty-something task force agent of Arabic descent, sat beside Devin as they were driven toward the compound. He looked elegant and dapper in his perfectly tailored suit, though the day before he'd been in shirt sleeves and jeans as they'd hashed out their final plans and Devin's role in them for hours on end. Amir's fictitious dossier had been meticulously compiled by Interpol. He was Sheik Ali Samir Mahmood, a Qatar billionaire with homes around the world and a love of purebred Arabian horses.

Perhaps sensing Devin's jangling nerves, Amir put a hand on Devin's forearm. He spoke in a calm, measured tone. "Remember, just be yourself. You are my estate agent. This is your area of expertise. You've bought and sold properties similar to this a dozen times over the years. We're lucky to have you onboard, Mr. Lyons."

Devin tried to take comfort from Mr. Haddad's reassurances, and in fact it was true. He'd been quite successful in his real estate endeavors in Asia, and did have a solid and legitimate background. They'd decided to have him use his real identity, since the more authentic the setup, the more likely they were to succeed.

As the car drove along the winding, narrow roads that led to the estate, Devin offered a silent prayer to whatever gods might be listening. *Please let me find Leah. Please let her be there. Please let her be alive.*

Finally they arrived at a large wrought iron gate beside which stood an intercom mounted on a post. The driver, also an undercover Interpol agent, lowered his window and pressed a button on the intercom. "Sheik Ali Samir Mahmood," he said, as if just the man's name was enough, which apparently it was. The gate slid slowly open, and the Bentley eased through.

As they curved along the private road toward the cliffs on which the magnificent villa had been built, the turquoise waters of the Andaman Sea sparkled into magnificent view and then Devin saw the breathtaking horse sculpture garden he'd seen in aerial photos George had collected, and which Jaidee had described. He swallowed hard, his heart beating uncomfortably fast. They were actually in the compound. Leah might be only yards away from him.

They parked in front of the main house of the sprawling property that Devin knew from the specs was actually a series of six separate buildings. Sheik Mahmood, as Devin reminded himself to think of Amir, walked a little ahead of Devin up the broad stone pathway and up the stairs toward the huge double doors.

Before they had a chance to knock, the doors were swung open and there stood a tall, swarthy man with a shaved head and a goatee, a diamond stud in one earlobe, dressed entirely in black. "Good afternoon," he said, stepping back and waving them in to the large front hall. He looked down his rather long nose at Devin. "Welcome to the home of Yousef Khalil. I am Hasan Hijaz, his steward." He held out his hand.

"A pleasure," Devin lied, extending his own hand. "Devin Lyons, at your service." *His steward? What was the guy, a fucking king?* Devin hoped the instant dislike he'd taken to this *steward* didn't show on his face.

Turning toward Amir, Hijaz smiled, or at least lifted his lips in what approximated a smile, though to Devin his eyes seemed cold and cunning. They shook hands as well.

"I do hope you will forgive me, gentleman, but the prince is a man of great wealth and importance. We have to take precautions suitable to a man of his stature before allowing anyone into his midst."

During Devin's briefing, he'd been told that Khalil was a millionaire many times over, due to family money associated with oil, and also, no doubt, to his slave trafficking, but he was no prince. He liked to pass himself off as a distant cousin of the King Abdullah of Saudi Arabia, but no such bloodline existed.

Two short, muscle-bound men appeared behind Hijaz, their small, piggy eyes blank as they stared through Devin and Amir. "Please remove your jackets and lift your arms. These men are trained to do a quick but thorough search for weapons. And of course," Hijaz nodded toward the briefcase in Devin's hand, "We'll need to examine the contents of the case. Again, I do apologize for the unseemliness of this precaution, but I'm sure you understand…"

"Absolutely," Amir said crisply, slipping out of his suit jacket, which he handed to Hijaz. "I insist on the same at all my properties. One can't be too careful in these dangerous times." A sharp glance in Devin's direction made him hand over the money-stuffed briefcase to Hijaz. Then Devin shucked his jacket and, along with Amir, stood with arms out while the two men patted and frisked them from neck to ankle.

Hijaz moved out of his line of vision with the briefcase, but Devin could hear the clasps being clicked open. Would it faze Hijaz in the slightest to see all those bundles of cold, hard cash? Somehow Devin doubted it.

As Amir and Devin were putting their jackets back on, Hijaz returned, holding out the briefcase. "A regrettable formality," he said, training his cold, marble eyes on Devin.

Turning to Amir, Hijaz smiled and began to speak in Arabic. Amir responded in kind. Devin, who had a rudimentary knowledge of the language, was able to discern that they were exchanging pleasantries and making comments and inquiries about each other's health and the health of their respective families.

Finally Hijaz led them through a large, elegantly appointed living area and up a flight of wide, thickly carpeted stairs. They were taken to the end of a hallway and through an open door. One wall of the room was entirely of glass, opening onto a stunning view of the sea lapping against the white sand of the shore. On a pedestal in front of the window stood an exquisitely rendered white marble sculpture of a horse rearing back on its hind legs, its mane flying—a miniature of the life-size horses displayed in the estate gardens.

A man stood with his back to them, staring out at the ocean view, his hands clasped behind his back. As they entered the room, he turned to face them. He was wearing a white silk shirt over loose-fitting red silk pants, his feet clad in tan leather sandals. He was tall and lean, with an elegant hooked nose, a full mouth and lots of dark, wavy hair. Devin recognized the man was handsome but something about him put Devin off. Perhaps it was the intensity of his large dark eyes as they moved restlessly over the two men. There was a kind of coiled, dangerous energy in the man that made Devin's hackles rise, despite his movie star smile.

Hijaz bowed slightly in the direction of the man. "May I present Sheik Ali Samir Mahmood and his estate agent, Devin Lyons. Gentlemen, this is Yousef Khalil, my lord and master."

Lord and master? That was a bit much, Devin thought, even giving allowance for the fake title of prince and the flowery language of traditional Arabic greetings.

The man nodded toward Hijaz in a way that told Devin he took the appellation as his due. Turning toward Amir and Devin, he said, "Welcome to my humble abode, gentlemen." His accent was pure Oxford. He strode toward them, shaking hands with each, placing his second hand on top as they shook.

Gesturing toward a grouping of chairs, he indicated that the men should sit. Devin had expected Hijaz to join them, but he said, "I will see to your refreshments, gentleman," and, with another bow, left the room.

Amir and Khalil began the customary and, to Devin's mind, very lengthy exchange of greetings and discussion of familial health that was necessary in polite Arabic society. They spoke in English for Devin's sake.

"I understand you are an admirer of horses," Khalil finally said, and off the two went, discussing their mutual love of all things equine, while Devin silently chafed.

"Excuse me," he wanted to say. "You two keep chatting. I'll just go off and have a look for the cells where you keep the kidnapped women, shall I?"

Instead, he extracted the thin portfolio from his suit jacket that contained the fake contract for the sale of the property, along with the special pen Interpol had provided. He depressed the small button on the side of the pen that activated the microphone and recording device, and placed it and the portfolio on the coffee table.

He half expected Khalil to grab the pen and fling it across the room in a rage, or worse, pull out a gun and shoot them both on the spot. But he only went on talking to Amir about the superiority of Arabian purebreds, gesturing with his long, elegant hands as he made his point.

The two men's discourse was interrupted by a short, thin man in a white shirt and black pants who carried a tray containing a brass samovar, three tiny coffee cups and a plate of pastries. Khalil made a big deal about pouring the coffee himself, watching with dark, expectant eyes until they had tasted it. Devin forced himself take a sip, though his stomach was roiling with nerves.

After they drank the strong, sweet coffee and nibbled pastry for a while, Amir finally said, "As I discussed with your man, I am prepared to pay a significant sum for this stunning property. The horse sculptures alone are enough to seal the deal. I know you say you aren't interested in selling, but I am hopeful we can come to a mutually satisfactory agreement."

He leaned forward, his tone dropping into something conspiratorial. "You see, I'm familiar with the blueprint of the buildings. I'm especially concerned with proper quarters for my women. I want somewhere they can be sequestered, you understand. Kept safe from the prying eyes of the servants and guests. And of course, I keep my women under strict control. I don't hold with this modern nonsense about women's rights. What does that even mean? A woman exists solely to serve a man, don't you agree?"

Khalil raised his eyebrows, his mouth lifting in a genuine smile. "Indeed I do. Women don't have the natural intelligence and understanding of a man. They must be taught, especially today's modern woman, that their place is at the feet of their man. If sometimes that lesson is at the end of a whip…" He shrugged, his eyes glinting as he added, "Firm discipline is essential." He licked his red lips, his dark eyes flitting from Amir to Devin. Devin wanted nothing more than to smash his face in.

"Quite," Amir asserted, playing his part perfectly. "Aside from the glorious sculpture garden," he gushed, "that is the one thing that most struck me about this villa." He leaned forward, his hands on his knees, his expression intent. "I need a common room for my women, and then of course a separate chamber for each. Mr. Lyons, who has reviewed the blueprints meticulously, assures me you have the proper accommodations for easily five women, quite apart from the rest of the house."

Khalil smiled. "I am glad to see you share my philosophy regarding a woman's role." He turned to Devin. "And you, Mr. Lyons. How refreshing to find a Westerner who is not judgmental about ancient cultures, and can appreciate that our ways have worked well for us over thousands of years."

Devin nodded and tried to smile, not trusting himself to speak. Khalil turned back to Amir. "Alas, my dear friend, I am content here. I have made this my home. I am sure you appreciate that I hadn't considered selling. I extended the courtesy of a visit out of respect to a fellow Arab, but I'm quite happy here, sir. Quite happy, indeed."

Amir had told Devin that sources indicted Khalil had in fact been putting out initial feelers for a new location. He never stayed anywhere for more than a few years at a time, no doubt to keep one step ahead of the law with his slave trafficking operations. But Amir only said, "Quite. I do understand. You are a man of refinement—someone who appreciates beauty in all its forms."

Khalil nodded in a smug, self-congratulatory way that made Devin's knuckles actually itch as he fantasized landing a solid right on that handsome, square jaw. "Nevertheless," Amir went on smoothly, playing his part to the hilt. "I sense you are also a man of business. A man who doesn't hesitate to seize an opportunity when it is presented."

He paused and spread his hands, palms upward, in Khalil's direction. "I am prepared to offer twice the market value. My agent, Mr. Lyons has drawn up a contract. We'll leave it for your review, along with the money in that briefcase as a gesture of my good faith." He nodded toward the case, which sat at Devin's feet.

Khalil said nothing. He lifted his tiny coffee cup and took a sip. Amir, too, lifted his cup. He glanced at Devin, giving him a nearly imperceptible nod.

Devin took his cue, as they'd planned the night before, and stood. "If you would be so kind, may I use the facilities?"

"Of course. Just through that door." Khalil gestured toward a small door on the side of the room. Devin stepped through it into a bathroom, pulling the door shut behind him.

He could hear the two men murmuring on the other side of the door, and knew they were speaking in Arabic. Amir was now moving in for the kill, trying to get the guy to spill the beans. His plan was to insinuate that he himself was in the market for a slave girl or two, and, as a fellow Arab, would appreciate any light Khalil might be able to shed on the process.

Devin stared at himself in the bathroom mirror, surprised that he appeared calm, though his heart was jumping and his intestines were twisted into knots. Leah might be close by, chained in some dungeon, or locked in some harem with a dozen other women. He refused to entertain the possibility that she wasn't here. His desire—his *need*—to find her, to rescue her, outweighed any possibility of failure.

He lingered as long as he dared in the bathroom to give Amir enough time, before finally opening the door and returning to the room.

Amir turned to him, saying the words that let Devin know he'd fooled the man into believing he was in the market for human flesh. "Mr. Lyons, if you will forgive us, my dear friend and I have something private to discuss. I'm sure you understand." He gave an imperious wave of his hand. "You may wait in the car until I have further need of your services."

"I'll have an escort show you to the door," Khalil added.

You wouldn't want me stumbling on the slave quarters, now would you? Having no choice, Devin allowed one of the men who had frisked him to lead him back through the house and to the front door. Outside, the policeman posing as their chauffeur was leaning against the car drinking a bottle of orange soda. As Devin approached, he straightened up smartly and opened the back door for Devin. Devin slipped into the backseat.

The man slid into his seat in the front, pulling the door closed behind him. Without turning around, he said, "He's in?"

"Yes," Devin replied.

They sat in silence, waiting. Devin closed his eyes and counted slowly to one hundred. Then he did it again. When he was on eighty-six, he heard a beeping sound from the front seat. Amir's mobile phone had a GPS tracking device on it. He was to give a signal when he was in the quarters where the abducted women were being held.

The driver pulled a mobile phone from his breast pocket and punched in a series of numbers. "Ten minutes," he said.

They were the longest ten minutes Devin ever experienced. Amir and that motherfucking bastard Khalil might at that very moment be in a room with his beloved Leah, and he was sitting here like a jerk in the back of this car.

Finally he heard the droning sound of approaching helicopters. Within seconds they had landed on the perfectly manicured lawns on either side of the circular drive, the whirring blades slashing the air. The doors opened and a half a dozen men dressed in black uniforms, guns in hand, came swarming from each 'copter.

Though Devin had been told to stay put, he found himself opening the door and tumbling from the car. There was no way he could sit idly by while the rescue was going down. The men moved quickly. About half of them battered their way into the main house, while the rest took off to other parts of the compound, weapons at the ready.

Devin ran behind the uniformed men through the door of the main house. The man in front of him turned, barking something sharply in Thai as he pointed his weapon at Devin. Devin froze.

The commander, a man who had been at the meetings at headquarters when Devin was being briefed for his part in the sting, turned back and said something in Thai to the man, who lowered his weapon. To Devin, he said, "I told him you're cleared. But make sure you stay behind the men. Don't do anything stupid. There are lives at stake."

Devin nodded. The commander was holding a tracking device that presumably would lead them to Amir and the women. "This way!" he shouted, sprinting toward the stairs. The men thundered up the stairs and ran along a labyrinth of hallways to another set of stairs. Devin was right behind them, spurred on by adrenaline.

They burst into a room, halting just inside the door. The commander called out in Thai, Arabic and finally English, "Po-lice! Freeze!" as he aimed his weapon at Khalil and Amir. Khalil stared open-mouth at the men and then stood, slowly lifting his hands above his head. His eyes slid toward Amir, shock, realization and then fury moving over his face in quick succession.

He had been sitting in a large, throne-like chair, Amir standing beside him. In front of them a young woman was kneeling with her head on the floor, her back toward the door, arms stretched along the floor in front of her head.

"Leah!" Devin cried, before he could stop himself. The girl rose with a cry, and Devin saw it was not Leah at all, but a smaller, slighter woman with long, dark hair. She was clearly naked beneath gauzy veils that were artfully draped over her body. There were thick gold bracelets around her wrists and ankles, and a thin gold collar around her neck.

While the police entered the room and swarmed over Khalil, cuffing his hands behind his back, the girl locked eyes with Devin and whispered, "Leah." She pointed toward a small door at the back of the room.

Aware he was going to get into all kinds of trouble with Amir and Interpol, Devin pushed his way past the hubbub and reached the door. He slid back the bolt and turned the knob. Opening the door, he slipped inside, his heart beating high in his throat.

~*~

Leah tossed in the bed, unable to get comfortable. She felt weak and spent, literally beaten down by the horrific events of the past few days. How much longer could she go on like this? Would she come to accept and even embrace her lot, as Naeemah seemed to? Or, more likely, would she just lose her mind and become a zombie, going through the motions, doing whatever it took to avoid pain and seek what pleasure was offered.

This horrible specter, as much as the pain, kept her from sleeping. By her calculations, this was her fourth day. Hadn't she heard somewhere that the first twenty-four hours were the most crucial? She knew as each day passed, the odds of her being found and rescued dwindled. Would she end up just another statistic, another unaccounted for missing person?

No. Don't think that way. Don't give up. Devin knows you're missing. Devin will find you. Leah sighed, not sure if she believed this anymore or not, but what else did she have to cling to?

If only her body didn't ache so. She was bruised and battered, and it wasn't only the brand that was hurting. The steward had awakened her not long after Naeemah's visit, furious that she hadn't properly reciprocated the young woman's attentions. Apparently, the creepy bastard and his fucking boss had been watching the girl-on-girl action the camera had recorded, and they were pissed Leah hadn't gone down on the girl.

The steward had yanked her from the bed and thrown her to the floor, using a riding crop to smack every inch of her naked body, while also kicking her with the sharp point of his boot. He'd been careful to avoid the brand—no doubt not daring to mar Khalil's mark of ownership. He'd left her huddled in a corner, sobbing and shaking.

Alex came to her some time later, taking her for a soothing bath. Gently and carefully he cleaned and dressed the brand, and though he said nothing to her, she thought she saw the disapproval on his face. At least she hadn't been forced to see Khalil directly afterward, but was instead allowed to return to the small bedroom.

She was given a plate of sliced apples and a glass of water, but nothing more. She stared at the unblinking eye of the video camera as she ate, noting that the red light had been turned off. They only recorded when there was a show to see, apparently, the voyeuristic dickwads.

Leah must have dozed because she came awake suddenly to the sound of rumbling and clomping that got louder and louder, until she realized it was coming from right next door, through the door Naeemah had slipped through. There was shouting and commotion. She thought she heard the words, "Police! Freeze!" in English.

With a gasp, she grabbed the sheets and pulled them around her, her heart slamming in her chest. Someone was here! Someone had infiltrated the compound. She had to make sure they knew she was here too.

"Help!" she cried, but her voice came out as a choked whimper. She rolled from the bed, taking the sheets with her. Her body screamed its protest, still aching from the steward's brutal treatment, but she had to get up. She had to get to that door! She had to get it open.

As if she'd willed it, at that moment the door flew open, and Leah, startled, screamed.

A man stood there, silhouetted against the bright light behind him, which flooded into the bedroom, lit only by the single lamp near the bed. "Oh, my god. Oh,

Leah. It's you. It's you! I found you. My darling, you're alive."

Before Leah could process what was happening, the man advanced into the room and leaned down, lifting her into strong arms. It couldn't be real—she must be dreaming, and yet, and yet!

"Devin!" she breathed, pressing her face against his broad chest, tears of relief and joy coursing down her cheeks. "I knew you would come."

Chapter 12

Devin knocked lightly on the hospital room door, which was ajar. "Leah?" He pushed the door all the way open and stepped inside, aware he was holding his breath. She was sleeping, curled on her side like a golden angel, a white hospital gown over her shoulders. Her hair was pulled back in a ponytail, and her long, thick lashes brushed her cheeks.

The nurse had told him she was dehydrated when they brought her in, but other than some slight malnutrition, some bumps and bruises, and the burn on her back, she was in excellent condition. An IV drip, a few good meals and plenty of rest had made a huge difference, the nurse told him.

Devin had seen the bandage on her back when he'd scooped her into his arms during the rescue. She'd been crying too hard to explain, clinging to him and kissing his face through her tears. He hadn't wanted to press her then, nor had there been time, even if he'd wanted to. He'd wrapped her in a blanket and held her close, letting her cry.

One of the task force officers had entered the small bedroom moments after Devin. Using a walkie talkie, he called for two medics, giving his location. Not long after, two men carrying a stretcher came bursting into the room. Leah didn't want to let go of Devin, nor he of her, but he'd given her one last kiss and whispered, "They're going to take to you to hospital. I'll be right behind, I promise."

Leah, along with three other young women, had been whisked away by helicopter, taken to Bumrungrad Hospital in Bangkok for evaluation. Devin tried to stay out of the way while Khalil, Hajiz, the two burly guards and several other men were handcuffed and loaded into the large police van that had arrived on the premises.

Amir had left with the police, while Devin had been driven back to Interpol headquarters in Bangkok, where he was debriefed, as they called it. Basically, he had been thanked for his assistance in the operation, and then lectured about civilians sticking their neck out and risking the safety of all involved in a police operation.

As soon as he could get away, he had hightailed his way to the hospital, only to be stonewalled there because Leah was in a high security ward, with no visitors allowed. By sweet talking a nurse on a nearby unit, he was able to get information as to Leah's general health, which was good overall, the nurse had reassured him.

He spent the night in a nearby hotel, watching a strange Thai movie with English subtitles on the television until he fell asleep, sometime near dawn. Amir had pulled a few strings after the twenty-four hour observation period, procuring a family visitor's pass for Devin, once he'd gotten Leah's okay.

Amir had warned Devin about the brand on Leah's back, explaining that the branding of women abducted by slave traffickers wasn't all that unusual. It was a way to stake a claim, marking the prostitute or slave as property. Devin shuddered to think of Leah being subjected to such brutal, dehumanizing treatment. At least she'd only been held for four days. Imagine if they hadn't acted fast enough, and Khalil had disappeared before they got there, taking Leah with him.

Now Devin sat in the visitor's chair beside Leah's bed, drinking in the sight of her. He had never permitted himself to think she'd been killed, not while she was missing, but now, staring down at her, he realized how incredibly lucky they had been to find her at all, and to find her alive.

He wanted to lean over and scoop her into his arms. He wanted to enfold her into him and keep her safe always. At the same time, he was almost afraid to touch her, as if she might shatter on contact. She looked so fragile lying there.

When she woke up, would she be glad to see him? They'd known each other for all of a day before the horrendous abduction. It was possible she'd want nothing to do with him after this. It was possible she couldn't wait to get on the next flight to the States, putting this nightmare behind her, Devin included.

Leah sighed in her sleep and her eyelids fluttered open. "Leah," Devin said gently, not wanting to startle her. "Hi, there," he added inanely as she fixed him with those startlingly blue eyes.

"Devin." She reached out a hand and instinctively he leaned closer. She stroked his cheek, her eyes pooling with tears. "Devin," she said again, the word like a caress.

"Leah," he replied, blinking back his own tears as he smiled at her, his heart swelling.

Turning slightly, Leah lifted herself on her elbows. Devin stood, reaching to plump the pillows behind her. She winced as she leaned back against them.

Alarmed, Devin said, "You okay? Should I get the nurse?"

"No, no, I'm fine. A little sore, but I'm good." She smiled at him. "Sit down. I've had enough of people clucking around me. Just sit down and let me look at you, Mr. Bond."

Devin grinned at the reference to his looking like Sean Connery, for a moment transported back to that first day on the beach, and the light, sexy banter that had gone on between them. Would they be able to get back to that sweet, easy place?

He sat, a million questions burning on his lips about what she'd been through. Instead he said, "How's the food in this place?"

She smiled. "Not bad. They bring me meals like every twenty minutes. The nurse is worse than my mom."

"Speaking of," Devin said. "Have you contacted your parents? Are they flying in?" In his mind, Devin had already decided Leah would be on the first plane out of Asia as soon as she was released and given clearance by Interpol. He realized he didn't even know what state she lived in. He knew next to nothing about this girl, other than that she had occupied most of his brain and all of his heart since the moment he'd met her.

"God, no," Leah said emphatically. "I haven't told them. They would shit bricks. My dad would go nuts with the *I told you so* lecture about a young woman traveling abroad and my mother would just cry and fix me with her mournful cow's stare. That's all I don't need, thank you."

"Oh!" Devin said, genuinely surprised. "I just assumed—"

"That because I'm twenty-three and American, the first thing I'm going to do is run home to mommy and daddy?" Leah interrupted, her lovely eyes flashing with the spark that had first attracted him. "It's my money, not theirs, and my life."

Devin couldn't suppress a grin. Leah was her feisty self, or so it seemed. "My apologies, Ms. Jacobs. I meant no offense."

Leah shook her head, a sheepish smile moving over her face. "Hey, I'm sorry. The Interpol guys keep asking me about my parents, and when they're coming for me, like I'm twelve or something. Do I want to get out of Thailand? Hell yeah. But not so I can go running into the arms of my parents. I was thinking..." She paused several beats, fixing Devin with a bold stare, though it was belied by the color creeping up her cheeks. Reaching back, she tugged at the elastic holding her hair back and wound the long, silky golden strands around her fingers.

"I haven't been to London for some time," she finally said. "Amir's getting a replacement passport for me at the embassy. Know of any cheap flights out? Oh, and I would need a place to stay."

~*~

Three Weeks Later

"What're you doing?"

Leah whipped her head away from the mirror and toward the sound of Devin's voice, making no attempt to cover her naked body. Devin stood in the bathroom doorway wearing only his silk boxers, looking, as he always did to Leah, good enough to eat with a spoon. Only forget the spoon.

"I was looking at the brand in the mirror," she admitted. The burn was healing well, so the doctors said. The skin was still covered in ugly scabs, but that was to be expected as a normal part of the healing process. It could take up to a full year to completely heal, eventually fading to a ridge of pink or white, the intensity of the color dependent on the amount of pigment in the skin.

"I hate how you got it," Devin said, moving close and pulling her into his arms. "But I think of it as a badge of courage."

"A what?"

Devin looked into her eyes, his face blazing with tenderness. "A badge of courage. A wound sustained in a war. Something you can carry with pride, because you didn't give up, Leah. You kept up your courage. They might have controlled your body, but you didn't let them take your dignity or your pride."

Leah smiled. "It didn't feel like that at the time. It was just a matter of survival, I guess. It's not like I had a lot of choice in the matter."

"You chose to keep your wits about you and you didn't let them break your spirit. A lot of people would have broken down under that kind of pressure. You didn't."

She looked into Devin's earnest, handsome face. "And you didn't give up on me, either. You refused to believe I'd just gone off to Bangkok, like that creep tried to make you think."

"After what we had shared, I knew you wouldn't do that, Leah."

Leah reached up, stroking Devin's cheek. "I used to dream of you at night. That somehow you would find me and come for me." She circled her arms around his neck, pulling him down for a kiss. "And you did. Somehow, you did."

They kissed for a long time and then Devin led her back into the bedroom of his London garden flat, which they'd barely left since arriving. They'd spent most of their time eating, sleeping and making love. When they weren't doing that, they were talking, endlessly processing what had happened for each of them during the horrific four days Leah had been held captive.

At first Leah had been hesitant to tell Devin the details of her time at the compound, afraid of both his reaction, and her fear of reliving it through the telling. But he'd been so gentle and easy to talk to that once she started, she hadn't been able to stop. It was like peeling an onion, pulling away the layers of pain and terror she'd endured. And as she poured out the story, it felt somehow as if she could toss the layers aside in the telling, their sting and power lessened by exposure.

True, she still woke sometimes in the night, her heart racing, sweat pouring from her body, caught in a nightmare where she was running, desperate to escape, only to find herself again and again back in that crawl space beneath the stairs, or hanging from a hook, a whip slicing the skin from her back in long, painful strips while she howled.

She would wake crying, or gasping for air and always, always, Devin was there, his strong arms encircling her as he whispered, "You're okay, baby. You're safe now. It's all okay."

She wanted him to be right. She needed for it to all be okay. She told herself over and over that she was free.

She was safe. Everything was fine. And for the most part, she believed it. But could it ever really be fine? Would she ever get past the nightmares and the horrific memories? And what about all the women and girls still enslaved? Just because Yousef Khalil's operation had been shut down, there was still a world of evil out there.

She'd learned a huge lesson and knew she would be far more careful in her future travels, but despite what others might think, or how they might have reacted, it hadn't dampened her wanderlust. Though just now, at this moment, all she wanted was to stay cocooned with Devin, eating the wonderful cupcakes he brought from the Hummingbird Bakery and the delicious Indian food from the local corner market, and making love until they fell asleep in a tangle of legs and arms.

"Hey, you put new bedding on while I was in the bath," Leah said, plopping down on the fresh, white sheets of Devin's king size bed.

"I did," he admitted, smiling. "In honor of your first whipping."

"My what?" Leah stilled, though her heart picked up its pace. She'd been asking over the past few days when they would reintroduce BDSM into their lovemaking. At first she'd agreed with Devin that they should take it easy and be careful while her brand was healing, but as the days passed, she found herself longing for more than vanilla sex with only a dash of spice. She wanted the full treatment.

"You heard me, sexy girl. Your first whipping." Devin pulled open a drawer of his bureau and withdrew a coiled whip, similar to the one she'd seen in Pattaya, though the lash wasn't as long and it had ended in a nylon cracker.

"Some call it a single tail, but the proper term is signal whip," Devin said, running his fingers along the braided leather. "Because it's shorter, it's more suitable for indoor use than the bullwhip you saw in Pattaya." Letting it unfurl, he snapped it in the air, the cracking sound drawing a startled gasp from Leah, not to mention a sudden, sharp tug in her pussy.

He moved to her, gently pushing her flat onto the bed. She lay back willingly, her nipples suddenly aching and hard. He dragged the long, soft leather thong over her breasts, stomach and thighs. Leaning over her, he grazed her neck with his lips, sliding lower to tease her nipples with a gentle, sensual flick of his tongue.

"Have you ever experienced a whipping with one of these?" Devin drew the tail over her body, resting the handle between her legs, which, somehow, had fallen open.

Leah moaned. "No," she whispered huskily. "I've always wanted to experience it. I know it can be very intense."

Devin's smile was almost evil, though his golden brown eyes were sparkling. "Bullwhips and signal whips aren't something you just pick up and use. But in the right hands, they're as sexy as they are dangerous.

The lash can create a range of sensations from delicate to cruel."

He lifted the lash, lightly stroking its deceptively soft nylon tip over her skin. "It can be as subtle as a lover's tongue or as sharp as a blade." Leah licked her lips and closed her thighs around the hard whip handle, feeling the swell of her pussy lips against it.

"In the hands of an expert," Devin continued, sliding onto the bed and stretching out beside her, "a well-made whip becomes a living thing, much in the way a Samurai warrior's sword vibrates with the life force given to it by the master sword maker. But what really makes the experience come alive is the interaction of the partners — that connection, that oneness between two, that kindred pairing that allows pleasure and erotic pain to flow freely from the giver to the receiver and back again."

"Yes," Leah whispered, "I understand."

And she did understand, not only intellectually, but also on a gut level, that what he was offering had nothing to do with the beatings she'd received at the hands of the guards at the compound, or even that much in common with the BDSM play she'd engaged in at the clubs and with previous lovers. For while that kind of play had been fun and exciting, a key element had always been missing. She understood that now.

"Are you ready, Leah? Are you ready to suffer for me?"

The words had a power of their own, and Leah felt her body softening and opening. "Yes," she whispered fervently.

He kissed her cheek and nodded, rising from the bed. "I want you to lie flat on your stomach. I'm going to tie you down, not only for the erotic aspect of bondage, but also to keep you safe. With a whip like this, you don't want your subject squirming around. A misplaced strike could cut your skin. Safety is as important as pleasure when it comes to the art of the whip."

Leah lay quietly as Devin retrieved several lengths of thin nylon rope from his toy drawer. She lay still as he took her wrists, one at a time, and then her ankles, winding the soft rope snuggly in place, and then securing it to the legs of bed, forcing her body into an X and pulling her down into the mattress.

She was quiet, but anything but passive. Her heart was thumping, her breath already ragged with excitement. She felt taut in her position, the ropes stretching her limbs, though not uncomfortably. Her skin tingled from head to toe, electric with the need to feel the signal whip's burning kiss. At the same time, she felt that deep, velvet cocooning sense of contentment and safety that being bound in rope always engendered in her.

The fact that it was Devin Lyons, her beloved Devin, standing beside her made it all the more meaningful. She trusted him with her heart, her soul, her very life. She was ready, more than ready, for this new experience and despite her fear, perhaps partially because of it, every nerve ending thrummed with aching anticipation.

"Leah." Devin knelt beside the bed, his mouth close to her ear. "Are you comfortable? Are the ropes good?"

"Yes."

"Are you sure you want this? Because you can say no. We have all the time in the world, darling. If it's too soon—"

"No!" Leah interrupted. "I want it. I do. More than anything. Please."

She felt his hand moving over her back and ass, his touch gentle. His fingers slid down the crack between her cheeks, grazing her spread pussy. He pushed a finger inside her. It slipped in easily and Leah felt her muscles clamping down with desire.

Devin chuckled softly. "How did I know that's what I would find? You're soaking wet and we haven't even started yet."

Leah felt herself blushing, but she was grinning too. She couldn't deny it—she was more turned on than she'd ever been in her life, and more than ready for the erotic whipping Devin had promised.

He started by popping the whip over her head, its sonic crack making her body jerk, but when the cracker touched her skin, he only brushed it, feather soft, against her thigh. He made it crack again, and again brushed her thigh.

The first real strike landed on her ass, preceded a fraction of a second by a breeze caused by the cracker, followed by a slight sting. After several of these strokes, which were easy to tolerate, came a sudden burning stroke that made Leah yelp.

It had the slow burn of a cane strike, but with a more immediate bite, the focus on a smaller surface area perhaps accounting for the intensity. This was followed by several burning pops in a row that had Leah squirming in her bonds, though all she could really do was clench the ropes at her wrists and curl her toes.

He kept the focus on her ass and the backs of her thighs, though occasionally the whip curled, the tip making contact with her inner thigh, so close to her spread pussy that she felt the puff of air against her clit in the millisecond before the leather made contact with her leg.

Devin was out of her line of sight, but she felt him beside her, and then his fingers, which moved lightly over her burning ass, again dropping between her legs. She couldn't help herself—she pressed wantonly against his hand, trying with her very restricted mobility to push her cunt against him.

Again his sexy, throaty chuckle. "You doing okay?" he asked, pushing two fingers into her wetness so that her only answer was a grunt of pure lust. He stroked her pussy for several delicious minutes, the heat in her ass and thighs mingling with the fire burning in her cunt.

"Oh, god," she moaned, teetering on the edge of an orgasm.

"Not yet," Devin said, withdrawing his fingers. "I'm not done with you."

He began to whip her again, alternating the sensations from feather-soft strokes to gently stinging kisses, all the way to the slow sweet burn of braided leather on skin, and everything in between, until she was gasping, moaning, crying and sighing, not sure if she could take another stroke, yet at the same time needing more, more and still more.

"Enough," Devin finally whispered, his mouth again close to her ear. "You did beautifully well, Leah. I'm so proud of you. You're amazing."

She wanted more. She wanted to lose herself completely in the exquisite sensation he'd woven around her like a magical spell. "More," she managed to murmur. "More."

Devin kissed her cheek. "No, sweetheart. You're at the point where you'll let me flay you alive. You're in that place, that beautiful, peaceful place where you lose the ability to make good judgments about your tolerance for pain."

She felt him sitting beside her on the bed, though he made no move to untie her. Instead, she felt his hand moving down her back, the fingers lightly brushing the burning flesh on her ass and slipping lower, dipping into her wetness, pulling a groan from her lips.

"You are so fucking sexy," he whispered, his voice suddenly ragged. His fingers were moving inside her and over her vulva all at once, the friction perfect, the combination amazing.

Her body began to tremble and then shake, an orgasm rising against his hand like a wave. Still his fingers flew, stroking like a cock and a tongue all at the same time. She felt she would have lifted from the bed had the ropes not been holding her in place. As the climax took her over, she heard a strange, keening wail, and realized it was she, even her voice out of control as she careened over the edge of the most intense orgasm of her life.

Leah lay in a near-stupor, unable to move a muscle, not even her lips, not even her eyelids. She was aware of Devin moving briskly around her, untying the ropes and massaging her calves and arms to make sure her blood was flowing. She felt him lying down beside her, and then his strong arms reaching beneath her and gently flipping her onto her side.

He spooned her from behind, his warm body nestling against her, his hands gently cupping her breasts as he kissed her neck. She murmured something incoherent and he whispered, "Shh, don't try to speak. Just rest."

She did, drifting in and out of consciousness as she slowly came down to earth. "Wow," she finally said. "That was fucking *amazing*."

Devin chuckled softly. "You're a natural, Leah. You were born for the whip."

Leah smiled, pleased with this assessment. "It was..." she paused, trying to find the words to describe the intensity of what she'd experienced. "I don't know. Sublime is the word that comes to mind. Is that too corny?"

"Not at all," Devin said. He rolled onto his back, gently pulling her along with him. She turned toward him, curling into his side and resting her cheek on his smooth chest. "That's the difference between what we shared just now, and the so called scenes you can find at any BDSM club," Devin said. "They might be doing exactly the same thing, but the experience moves from the mere fun, to the sublime."

Leah lifted her head, looking into Devin's lovely golden brown eyes. "Why do you think that is? What accounts for such a huge difference?" Even as she asked it, all at once, she knew. Devin, she could tell, knew it too.

"Love," they said at the same time.

Then they laughed, the same gut wrenching, soul freeing belly laughs they'd shared that very first day on the beach. And Leah knew, as Devin took her again into his arms, that everything truly was going to be fine.

Just fine.

Also Available at Romance Unbound Publishing

(http://romanceunbound.com)

Caught
Slave Academy
Tough Boy
Enslaved
Princess
Heart Thief
Slave Island
Alternative Treatment
Switch
Dream Master
The Cowboy Poet
Safe in His Arms
Heart of Submission
The Solitary Knights of Pelham Bay – The Series
Texas Surrender
Unleashed Magic
Sarah's Awakening
Wicked Hearts
Submission Times Two
Confessions of a Submissive
A Princely Gift
Accidental Slave
Slave Girl

Lara's Submission
Slave Jade
Obsession: Girl Abducted
Golden Angel: Unwilling Sex Slave
The Toy
Frog: A Tale of Sexual Torture

Connect with Claire

Website: http://clairethompson.net
Romance Unbound Publishing: http://romanceunbound.com
Twitter: http://twitter.com/CThompsonAuthor
Facebook: http://www.facebook.com/ClaireThompsonauthor

Made in the USA
San Bernardino, CA
11 June 2016